Praise for

Breadcrumbs

Publishers Weekly Best Book

School Library Journal Best Book

Bulletin Blue Ribbon (*The Bulletin of the Center for Children's Books*)

Chicago Public Library Best of the Best

Indiebound Indie Next List

Amazon.com Best Books of the Year

NPR Backseat Book Club Featured Selection

"Like a fairy-tale heroine, Hazel traverses the woods without a breadcrumb trail to save a boy who may not want to be saved in this multilayered, artfully crafted, transforming testament to the power of friendship."

—*Kirkus Reviews* (starred review)

"The evocative magical landscape, superbly developed characters (particularly dreamy, self-doubting, determined Hazel and lost Jack), and the piercing sadness of a faltering childhood friendship give this delicately written fantasy wide and lingering appeal."

—*The Bulletin of the Center for Children's Books*
(starred review)

"The creepy fantasyland that Hazel traverses uses bits from other Andersen tales to create a story that, though melancholy, is beautifully written and wholly original."

—*Publishers Weekly* (starred review)

"Although this is a fantasy, its grounding in psychological realism and focus on Hazel's feelings makes it a fine choice for readers who prefer realistic fiction. Ursu's multilayered, dreamlike story stands out from the fantasy/quest pack."

—*School Library Journal* (starred review)

"A strange, amazing, sad, thoughtful, one-of-a-kind original. You will find no other book out there quite like this one, no matter how hard you try."   —Elizabeth Bird, Fuse #8

"Devastatingly brilliant and beautiful throughout, Anne Ursu's *Breadcrumbs* shines like a gem. Ursu has sculpted a rich and poignant adventure that brings readers deep into the mysterious, magical, and sometimes frightening forests of childhood and change. This is storytelling graced with depth and filled with wonder. *Breadcrumbs* is one of those rare novels that turned me on my head, then sat on my heart and refused to budge."

—Ingrid Law, Newbery Honor author of *Savvy*

"In *Breadcrumbs*, Anne Ursu leaves a trail for us to follow into the dark woods of the school playground and the enchanted forest as Hazel goes in search of her dearest friend, Jack. The crumbs that lead us are stories, which point the way toward understanding and acceptance of loss and sorrow and change, and which shout to us of hope and friendship and love. This is a lyrical book, a lovely book, and a smart book; it dares us to see stories as spreading more widely, and running more deeply, than we had imagined."

—Gary D. Schmidt, Newbery Honor author of
The Wednesday Wars

"Anne Ursu's potent evocation of midwinter Minneapolis is memorable; so, too, is her evocation of that moment when you realize a dear friend may have outgrown you."

—*The Horn Book*

"Wonderfully distinct, delightfully told, and destined for a long life on the shelf." —*Wall Street Journal*

"This is a big-hearted story about friendship and adventure that might make you quiver with apprehension at times, but it will also leave you laughing out loud at Hazel's wry observations about life. *Breadcrumbs* also touches on both the things we shed and the wisdom we gain as we grow older—themes that will resonate with both younger and older readers." —NPR

Breadcrumbs

ALSO BY ANNE URSU

Breadcrumbs

Anne Ursu

Drawings by Erin McGuire

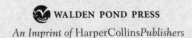

WALDEN POND PRESS

An Imprint of HarperCollins*Publishers*

Walden Pond Press is an imprint of HarperCollins Publishers.
Walden Pond Press and the skipping stone logo are trademarks and
registered trademarks of Walden Media, LLC.

Breadcrumbs
Text copyright © 2011 by Anne Ursu
Illustrations copyright © 2011 by Erin McGuire

Library of Congress Cataloging-in-Publication Data
Ursu, Anne.
Breadcrumbs / Anne Ursu ; drawings by Erin McGuire. — 1st ed.
p. cm.
Audience: Ages 8–12.
ISBN 978-0-06-201506-8
1. Magic mirrors—Juvenile fiction. 2. Friendship—Juvenile fiction.
3. Rescues—Juvenile fiction. 4. Children—Juvenile fiction.
[1. Magic—Fiction. 2. Mirrors—Fiction. 3. Best friends—Fiction.
4. Friendship—Fiction. 5. Rescues—Fiction. 6. Schools—Fiction.]
I. McGuire, Erin, ill. II. Title.
PZ7.U692Br 2011
813.6—dc22
[[Fic]]
2010045666
Typography by Carla Weise
12 13 14 15 16 LP/BR 10 9 8 7 6 5 4 3 2 1
❖
First paperback edition, 2013

For Jordan Brown

CONTENTS

PART ONE

PART TWO

Breadcrumbs

PART ONE

Chapter One

Snowfall

It snowed right before Jack stopped talking to Hazel, fluffy white flakes big enough to show their crystal architecture, like perfect geometric poems. It was the sort of snow that transforms the world around it into a different kind of place. You know what it's like—when you wake up to find everything white and soft and quiet, when you run outside and your breath suddenly appears before you in a smoky poof, when you wonder for a moment if the world in which you woke up is not the same one that you went to bed in the night before. Things like that happen, at least in the stories you read. It was the sort of snowfall that, if there were any magic to be had in the world, would make it come out.

And magic did come out.

But not the kind you were expecting.

That morning, Hazel Anderson ran out of her small house in her white socks and green thermal pajamas. She leapt over the threshold of the house onto the front stoop where she stood, ignoring the snow biting at her ankles, to take in the white street. Everything was pristine. No cars had yet left their tracks to sully the road. The small squares of lawn that lay in front of each of the houses like perfectly aligned placemats seemed to stretch and join together as one great field of white. A thick blanket of snow covered each roof as if to warm and protect the house underneath.

All was quiet. The sun was just beginning to peek out over the horizon. The air smelled crisp and expectant. Snowflakes danced in the awakening sky, touching down softly on Hazel's long black hair.

Hazel sucked in her breath involuntarily, bringing in a blast of cold.

Something stirred inside her, some urge to plunge into the new white world and see what it had to offer. It was like she'd walked out of a dusty old wardrobe and found Narnia.

Hazel stuck her index finger out into the sky. A snowflake accepted her invitation, and she felt a momentary pinprick of cold on the pad of her bare finger. She gazed at the snowflake, considering its delicate structure. Inside it was another universe, and maybe if she figured out the right way to ask, someone would let her in.

Hazel jumped as her mother's voice came from behind her. "Come inside," she said, "you'll freeze!"

"Look at the snow!" Hazel said, turning to show her glimmering prize.

Her mom nodded from the doorway. "It's amazing when you can see the patterns like that. Look at it. See the six sides? It's called hexagonal symmetry. A snowflake is made—"

People were always doing this sort of thing to Hazel. Nobody could accept that she did not want to hear about gaseous balls and layers of atmosphere and refracted light and tiny building blocks of life. The truth of things was always much more mundane than what she could imagine, and she did not understand why people always wanted to replace the marvelous things in her head with this miserable heap of you're-a-fifth-grader-now facts.

And then Hazel's mother said something brisk about getting her inside and something funny about someone calling child protection, followed quickly by a practical warning about getting to school on time and not making things worse there, and then Hazel saw her mom's head suddenly snap to the right, saw her eyes widen and her mouth open and heard some sound creak out, but before

Hazel could make sense of it all, she felt something hit the middle of her back with a *thwack*.

Ouch.

Hazel yelped and whirled around. There, on the front step of the house next door was a brown-haired, freckled boy packing another snowball and smiling evilly.

A grin broke out on Hazel's face. "Jack!" she hollered, and bent down to gather some snow.

"No you don't," said her mom, shooting a glance at the house next door. She reached over the threshold and placed her hand on Hazel's back to guide her back into the house.

"I'll get you later," Hazel called to Jack as she disappeared inside.

"Just try it!" Jack called back, cackling.

Hazel's mom closed the front door with a sigh. "Look at you. What were you thinking?"

Hazel looked down. She had clumps of snow hanging off her pajama legs. As she moved her head, snowflakes fell off of her hair. She seemed to be shivering, though she had not noticed the cold until now.

"Come on. You better get dressed. You'll be late."

She was late. Hazel walked out the front door, bundled sensibly now in her green jacket and knit gloves and red boots, to see the yellow school bus disappearing into the distance, its wide tracks scarring the snow-covered street, its puffing black smoke trespassing against the white sky. She blinked and looked toward the front window of her house where her mother's form was already seated at the desk on the other side. Now she felt the snow's bite against her ankles like a bad memory.

Chewing on her lip, Hazel unlocked the front door and went back into the house. Her mom looked up at her and let out a nearly imperceptible exhale.

"I'm sorry," Hazel said.

"I'll get my keys," her mother said.

In a few moments, their small white car was bursting out of the garage onto the thickly blanketed driveway. And then there was a crunching from the back tires, and they were stopped.

The car groaned. Her mother swore. The wheels spun, one moment, two—the car lurched forward and backward, and her mother swore even more colorfully, and then they were free.

It was a twenty-block drive to school, fourteen of them down a two-lane one-way street. As they moved toward school, the houses became bolder, sprouting second stories that stood uneasily in their rickety wooden frames. Hazel used to want a house like this—something beat-up and possibly haunted, with a dumbwaiter for passing messages, with hidden compartments that contained mysterious old books—but then she would not live next to Jack anymore, and that was not worth all the secret passages in the world.

The snow was coming down harder now, and Hazel's mother leaned forward in her seat as she drove, as if to will the car through it all. Shiny SUVs charged through the snow, whizzing past Hazel and the other small cars that crept along like scared animals.

Hazel's mom started pressing down on the brake long before they got to the big intersection where they were to turn left—the one with the gas station that Hazel and Jack biked to in the summers to spend their allowance on Popsicles and push-ups; where the bakery with the birthday cakes used to be before it became another gas station; where the burger place that her dad always took her to after T-ball games had been before it was replaced by the fast-food Mexican place that her mother said made everything taste like plastic and sadness—but that didn't stop them from skidding when they hit the patch of ice just in front of it. The car began to spin to the right, her mother wrenched the wheel and pumped her foot furiously on the brake, a horn bleated behind them, and from everywhere around them came a polyphony of screeching tires.

Hazel yelped a little, and the car skidded into the busy

intersection and stopped. A car swerved around them, and another, before someone finally stopped and waved them ahead. Her mom sucked in her breath, then straightened the car and joined the slow-moving group in the far lane. Hazel did not think this was the time to tell her she was, technically, running a red light.

"Ah, this car," her mom said, to no one in particular.

Hazel laid a hand on the gray dashboard as if to comfort it. A year ago her father had bought a new station wagon. Better for driving in these Minnesota winters, he had said. Safer for everyone. Suddenly, they, too, were charging through the snow, leaving all the little cars of Minneapolis to fend for themselves. But that was last year. Hazel did not mind, though; she had lived many years with this old car, she remembered all the dents, and she had no use for gleaming new station wagons—even if they did have anti-lock brakes.

As they pulled into the side street next to the school, Hazel's mom let out a long breath and squeezed the steering wheel—though whether out of the camaraderie bent of surviving hardship or out of some desire to strangle the car, Hazel was not sure. As for Hazel, she chewed some more on her lip, because that seemed the thing to do. Her mom's eyes fell on her. "Well," she said, releasing the wheel, "that was an adventure."

Hazel nodded, though her mom knew nothing of adventures.

"I know you didn't mean to miss the bus, Hazel," her mother added, her voice gentle. "But you've got to try to be practical for me, okay? You're a big girl, and I just can't be—"

Hazel nodded again.

"Okay, good. Listen, I'm having coffee at Elizabeth Briggs's after school. Why don't you come? I'll pick you up right from school."

Hazel squirmed. She did not want to argue with her mom, not now. But—

"I'm going sledding with Jack."

Actually, this was not strictly true. She and Jack had made no plans. But they didn't need to make plans, for there was a thick layer of snow on the ground and hills to sled down. Plus she owed him a good pounding with a snowball.

"I thought perhaps you'd like to go hang out with Adelaide," her mother continued, as if she had not spoken. "She's such a nice girl. I think you two would really get along, if you just gave it a chance."

"I have plans."

"I know, but you can sled with Jack another time. I think you should spend time with . . . other people."

Hazel flushed. *With girls,* her mother meant. She scowled slightly, and her guilt plummeted deep into the snow, burying itself where no one would find it. She mumbled her good-bye and hopped out onto the sidewalk before her mom could cancel any more of her pretend plans.

The air was filled with the smells of winter, and car exhaust, and the familiar sausage-y–maple syrupy wafting from the Burger King across the street. Hazel took a moment to inhale it all, to let the smells wash over her— not that they were particularly good, but it was one more moment that she didn't have to be in school.

This was Hazel's first year at Lovelace Elementary. After her father moved away over the summer, her mother explained that they didn't have the money to send her to the school she'd gone to since kindergarten and she would have to switch. Her old school had been very different. The classrooms didn't have desks. They called their teachers by their first names. Hazel tried that with Mrs. Jacobs on her first day at Lovelace. It did not go over well.

The good thing was she now went to the same school as Jack. The bad thing was everything else. Hazel did not like sitting at a desk. She did not like having to call her teacher Mrs. Anything. She did not like homework and work sheets and fill-in-the-blank and multiple-choice. It used to be that Hazel's teachers said things like *Hazel is so creative* and

Hazel has such a great imagination, and now all she heard was *Hazel does not do the assignment asked of her* and *Hazel needs to learn to follow school rules.*

So Hazel stood and gathered herself for another day of the things she did not do and the things she needed to learn, when a voice burst through the air. "Hey!" it said. "Crazy Hazy, are you coming to school today or what?"

Hazel grimaced. Tyler Freeman was walking behind her, sporting a Twins hat like it was exactly the thing to wear in a blizzard, like all the coolest kids in the Arctic wore baseball caps on particularly snowy days. His mom's minivan sped down the street behind him, ready to crush the snow.

"Miss the bus, Hazy?" he said, his voice taunting.

"Um, so did you," Hazel said, turning up her nose elegantly as if it were not filled with stale fast-food sausage.

"Whatever," said Tyler.

Hazel grumbled inwardly. Now she was either going to have to pretend there was something really urgent she had to do right there on the snowy sidewalk, or walk in with Tyler, who hated her because Jack hung out with her during recess now instead of him. She couldn't help it if she was more interesting. Tyler and his friend Bobby made it very clear that they blamed her for Jack's abdication of duty. They were sure she must have done something to Jack, because he never would have picked a *girl* over them if he had his wits about him.

Hazel was about to bend down and wrestle with a particularly intricate problem with her right boot when Tyler burst ahead of her and ran through the gate, his messenger bag trailing behind him.

Hazel watched him go. Everyone in the fifth grade had messenger bags, everyone but Hazel, who had not been cc'ed on that particular school-wide email. And by the time she figured it out on her own, it wasn't like she could have asked her mom for one.

She'd asked Jack, a week into school, why he hadn't told her. He frowned, looked at his own messenger bag, which he'd had for a year, and shrugged. "Who cares about stuff like that?" he asked.

Now, slinging her perpetually uncool backpack on her shoulders, Hazel headed through the tall fence, up to the side entrance that they were supposed to use if they were late, and buzzed to be let in. She held the door for a group of fourth-grade fellow stragglers, because she was a nice person, unlike some people.

Hazel was decidedly late, and she had endured enough days with Mrs. Jacobs to know how this was going to go. But that didn't stop her from pausing outside the classroom opposite the hall from her own and peering in the window.

There Jack was, as he always was, sitting in the third row at the end, close enough to the door that Hazel could grin at him and he could make a face back at her. She stood a step back from the window and thought in his direction as hard as she could, as she always did on days they could not walk from the bus to class together. One moment. Two. He would know she was there. He always knew she was there. And then his head turned and he saw her, and a slow grin spread across his face. He waggled his eyebrows at her like a giant goofball—and though she had never before known what it meant to waggle, she did now—it meant *I got you pretty good this morning* and *I bet you want to get me back* and *Just try it, Anderson* and *We're going sledding later, right?* And all the weight of Hazel's snow-dampened morning was gone.

She grinned back at him and raised her eyebrows—*Try it, I will, Campbell!*—and then turned to her own classroom, forgetting the dread she should feel entering it.

But as soon as she walked in, Mrs. Jacobs eyed her and shook her head in the way that we do with people who are terrible disappointments and made a big show of marking something in her book, and there was the snow again, dumped right on her shoulders.

The desks were in five perfect lines of six. If ever these lines strayed from perfect, if someone should move his by scooting backward too vigorously, or trying to get just the right angle to pass a note, Mrs. Jacobs got very cranky. The average Lovelace fifth grader could not differentiate this from her normal state, but Hazel was attuned to these kinds of subtleties. In Jack's classroom sometimes they moved their desks into one big circle or into small groups. This was not the sort of nonsense Mrs. Jacobs would brook. Hazel sometimes wondered if her teacher came from that planet at the end of *Wrinkle in Time* where everyone has to be exactly the same, except Mrs. Jacobs would have been too happy there to ever leave.

So, trying desperately not to disturb the universe, Hazel took her place in her usual desk, third row from the back, right next to the window where she liked it. And even though her desk was in a perfect row and a perfect column, like it should be, she knew if someone came into the classroom, some wizard or witch or psychic or somebody like that, he would gaze around the room with the certainty that something was out of place, something was an inch too far to the right, half an inch too far to the back, and his eyes would fall on her.

Hazel sat behind Molly and Susan, who never paid any attention to Hazel, at first because they were best friends and that kept them occupied, and then they stopped being best friends and that, too, kept them occupied. And so that was all right. She sat next to Mikaela, who was usually too busy aligning her many-hued highlighters to notice whatever thing it was that Hazel was doing wrong. And so that was all right. But she sat in front of Bobby and Tyler. And that was not all right.

And, of course, as soon as she sat down she heard a voice hissing behind her.

"Hazel, you're late!" Tyler whispered, voice full of fake concern. "You know, you really should try to get to school on time."

She turned to glare at him. He and Bobby were both snickering. "You guys are big goons," she hissed back.

"*Goons?*" said Susan. Next to her, Molly laughed. The girls glanced at each other, and it seemed Hazel's shocking uncoolness was the thing that would finally bring the two of them back together.

Hazel looked at her desk. *They're stupid,* Jack would say. *They're babies. Ignore them. Who cares what they think?* In her head, she peered through the glass window of Mr. Williams's class, Jack waggled his eyebrows, and she grinned.

Mrs. Jacobs began to talk, and soon everyone was ignoring Hazel in favor of taking notes on prepositions or percentages, so Hazel turned her attention where it most felt at home—out the window, letting Mrs. Jacobs's voice recede into the background with everything else.

The windows to their classroom looked out onto the street, and across to some apartments and a big pet-grooming place. Her class at her old school looked out on a small patch of woods, and Hazel had always thought that there was something magical about them, that it was the sort of place she and Jack were supposed to go into together. They would bring breadcrumbs, and they would cross through the line of trees to see what awaited them.

There was nothing magical at all about the things outside the window in Mrs. Jacobs's room, but it was still more interesting than the things happening in it.

And then, the drone of Mrs. Jacobs's voice stopped midsentence—and who knows, maybe that sentence was *You then move the decimal point two places, like so,* or else *Say it with me: aboard, above, about, across, around*—and Hazel heard a sound like something deflating. It was a sound she was familiar with. She turned her head reluctantly to the front of the room.

"Hazel Anderson," said Mrs. Jacobs, who was the thing that had deflated, "would you sit still?"

Somebody sniggered. From somewhere in the back of the room someone else sneered, "Yeah, *Hazel*," which was not the greatest insult ever, but one thing Hazel had learned at her new school was when it comes to insults it's the thought that counts.

Mrs. Jacobs looked at her with weary eyes, and Hazel froze. She was still like the snow-covered morning. She did not even breathe, at least very much. She was going to listen, she was going to try, because she was not a little kid anymore, because it was her job to sit still and listen to the teacher and we all have to do our jobs in this world, even if we don't like them very much.

"That's better, Hazel," said Mrs. Jacobs.

Another snigger.

Hazel felt her cheeks burn. She just could not seem to do things right. It would be so much easier if Jack were in her class. At least then there would be one part of the room where she belonged.

Her mother said it would be a good chance to make new friends. And she'd tried. The first day of school she'd gone right up to the other kids and started talking to them and they'd looked at her like she was offering to welcome them to the Lollipop Guild. She had not known until this year that she was different from everyone else. When they had drama, she was the only girl who volunteered for roles in the skits. When they had art, she was the only one who painted Hogwarts. When they did writing, she was the only one who made up stories about girls with magic swords and great destinies.

She felt like she was from a different planet than

her schoolmates, and maybe it was true. Hazel had been adopted when she was a baby. Her parents said they flew a long way to take her home with them because they loved her so much they would travel the galaxy to get her. They could have meant that literally.

On Lovelace Parents' Night, four weeks into the school year—which had been more than enough time for Hazel to realize that she was different—she'd walked into the classroom with her mother, and people looked. They looked from her to her mother and back to her. And Hazel, for the first time, saw what they saw. Her mother was white with blue eyes and light brown hair. Hazel had straight black hair, odd big brown eyes, and dark brown skin. People looked, and Hazel looked, too, and when she looked she realized that everyone else came in matching sets of one kind or another.

Hazel stood there, un-matching, and she thought, *Ah, this is it, I see now.*

But then Susan walked in with her parents. On Culture Day, Susan had stood before the class and wrote her Chinese name on the board and spoke of folding paper into birds and dragons dancing down the street. Hazel wondered at this girl who had not only a great variety of shoes, but culture, too. It was the sort of thing Hazel was supposed to have. Mrs. Jacobs had even asked her, the day before, if she would have anything to share for the class. But Hazel only had beat-up sneakers.

Susan was from China, but, as Hazel learned that night, her parents were not. Susan did not match. Hazel stared at the girl and her pale, proud parents, stared so long that Susan noticed. The girl turned and stared back, quizzically, a little accusing and a little fearful, as if to ask, *Is there something on my face or are you just a spaz?*

Hazel needed to explain, she needed to say something, because maybe Susan didn't realize it, maybe Susan thought she was alone, too. This was the sort of thing she knew she was not supposed to do, that it was not quite appropriate, and yet she could not help herself. She walked over to Susan and grabbed her shoulder.

"You're like me," Hazel whispered.

Susan gave her a look that clearly said, *I do not know what you think you are saying, but I am nothing like you.*

Hazel dropped her hand and slunk away.

So it wasn't that, either.

She still didn't know why she didn't fit. And she'd given up trying to figure it out.

Chapter Two

FAIRY TALES

When it was finally time for recess, Hazel burst out of her seat and flew to her jacket, accidentally bumping into Mikaela with such force she sent a pink highlighter clattering down the hallway. Hazel ran past the doorway where Mrs. Jacobs stood, and out onto the white fields where Mr. Williams's class already roamed in their winter puffiness.

The snow had stopped coming down now. But the ground was thick with it, and half the fifth graders of Lovelace Elementary hurled themselves into it while the other half lifted their feet in and out of it warily, like they were treading on some hostile alien moon.

And there was Jack, waiting for her by the big slide, as

he almost always was. Every few days he'd go play capture the flag or football with Bobby and Tyler and the other boys to keep them from getting sulky. Hazel was okay with that. She'd sit and read. He'd always come back.

"Hey," he said, grinning as she ran to him. "Have you recovered from my devious snowball attack?"

"Didn't even feel it!" chirped Hazel. "Got to work on your arm strength!"

"Not me," said Jack, molding a snowball in his hands. "You're pitching today."

He didn't have to say anything else. Hazel took the snowball and moved back.

Jack had moved in next door when she was six. She liked him right away because he replaced the girl who'd lived there before, a four-year-old who was always trying to convince Hazel to come to her tea parties, where no talking was allowed. Plus he was wearing an eye patch. Hazel's six-year-old self was sorely disappointed when she found out that he didn't actually need one, but she quickly learned it was the wearing one that really mattered. This was a secret truth about the world, one they both understood.

Jack was the only person she knew with an imagination, at least a real one. The only tea parties he'd have were ones in Wonderland, or the Arctic, or in the darkest reaches of space. He was the only person who saw things for what they could be instead of just what they were. He saw what lived beyond the edges of the things your eyes took in. And though they eventually grew out of Wonderland Arctic space-people tea parties, that essential thing remained the same. Hazel fit with Jack.

Today they were playing superhero baseball, which was a variation Jack had invented on the theory that superheroes, too, needed organized sports. The trick was they had to hide their superpowers, which is hard when you are so awesome at baseball.

Hazel was pitching snowballs, trying to keep her fastball from breaking a hole in the space-time continuum, while Jack hit the ball and jogged stiffly around the bases, pretending he ran like a man who had not been bitten by a radioactive mosquito.

"I got a new character for you," Jack said, whiffing at a snowball with his stick.

"You do?" Hazel let her arm fall to her side and took a step forward. "Can I see?" Jack was the best artist in the whole fifth grade. He'd been drawing ever since Hazel knew him, and for his birthday last year she'd gotten him this big fancy black sketchbook. He'd been using it to make up superheroes recently. Eventually he was going to make his own comic book. And Hazel was the only one who knew anything about it.

"Naw. Not outside. I'll show you on the bus. I was going to show you this morning, but you were too busy recovering from my snowball assault to get to the bus stop on time."

"Cool," Hazel said. "Can you tell me anything?"

"This one's a bad guy," Jack said. "They're more fun, you know?"

"What's he do?"

"I'll tell you later! Come on, are you pitching or what?"

"Sorry," Hazel said, taking a step back. "I'm going to throw a superhero curve, now."

"Yeah, I gotta learn to hit the curve if I'm going to be a baseball player when I grow up."

This was new. "What about comic books?"

"That, too. I can do both. You can't play baseball forever. I'm going to hit nine hundred home runs and get into the Hall of Fame."

"Nine hundred home runs? Is that a lot?"

Jack's eyes widened. "Is that a lot? No one's ever done that before. Not even guys who cheated! Or I could hit .400 a couple of times; that would do the trick. I'm going to be a great-hitting catcher like Joe Mauer."

Hazel just nodded and packed snowballs. She liked baseball, but Jack had the statistics of every player memorized, and that just was not good conversation in her opinion. Jack had even made imaginary stats for the superhero game.

Batman, oddly, had a lot of strikeouts.

Hazel wound up and pitched, and Jack smacked the snowball with the stick. It exploded into a jillion pieces. "Oops! Super strength!" Jack said, wiping the snow off his face.

Hazel lobbed a snowball at him. "Superhero baseball turns *evil*!" she called.

"Are you guys going out?"

Hazel whirled around. Mikaela and Molly were standing just behind her.

"Are you guys going out?" Molly repeated, her voice low and conspiratorial. She looked from Hazel to Jack, the snowballs to the stick, and raised her eyebrows.

At Lovelace Elementary, boys and girls who were together were "going out." At her old school they were just "going" or "going with," but at that point it wasn't something people actually did, just talked about a lot. Then it was okay for boys and girls to hang out together, but here none of the rest of the girls and boys did unless they were *together*, in which case they stood near each other, sometimes.

Someone asked Hazel this every once in a while, and she thought sometimes she should say yes, and then everyone would think she was the sort of person someone might like to go with, and that would be something. But she didn't want anyone to think it, not really. Jack was her best friend. And there was a time when everyone understood that, but they didn't anymore, because apparently when you get to be a certain age you're just supposed to wake up one morning and not want to be best friends with your best friend anymore, just because he's a boy and you don't have a messenger bag.

Hazel cast a glance at Jack, who was looking at her questioningly, his superhero bat dangling at his side, and then she straightened and tossed her black hair.

"Molly," she said, "you're a goon."

From the superhero batter's box came the sound of Jack cracking up. Hazel smiled. The girls' faces were identical masks of affront—because it was certainly bad enough to be called names when you were just innocently trying to be obnoxious, but far worse to be called something that, just an hour earlier, you had specifically established as dorky. They shook their heads, and then turned and walked away.

Thwack.

"Jack!" Hazel shouted, grabbing her shoulder where the snowball had hit.

The bell rang. Jack and Hazel fell in next to each other as they moved their way back into school, just a little separate from everyone else.

"So, you want to go sledding after school?" Jack asked.

"Yeah!" said Hazel. "But you gotta show me your drawing first."

"Promise," said Jack. "On the bus."

Hazel felt her heart lift. Jack usually sat in the back with the boys.

It wasn't until Hazel walked out of school and saw her mother's car parked across the street that she remembered that she wasn't going to be riding on the bus at all today. She had forgotten all about the plans her mother had made for her, had placed them in the box in her mind where things like *Take out the trash* and *Do the dishes* used to go, back when it was okay to forget about those things.

"Jack, I forgot. Mom's making me go with her somewhere. I can't go sledding."

Jack frowned. "Bummer."

"Yeah," Hazel said, eyeing him. He would never come out and say that he didn't want to go home, but she knew. "Can we go tomorrow?"

"Cool," said Jack.

They said good-bye, and Hazel grumbled her way to the car.

"Hi, dear!" her mother said brightly. "How was your day?"

Well, Tyler called her Crazy Hazy again and she was really late and Mrs. Jacobs wrote something in her book and people sniggered at her and you can't say "goon" and Molly's going to hate her now and she didn't get to ride home on the bus with Jack to make it all okay and he wanted to go sledding with her so he didn't have to go home and she's abandoning him even though she's his best friend and isn't supposed to do that ever ever ever.

"Okay," Hazel said.

Hazel could sense the familiar feeling of her mother's eyes on her. She looked ahead impassively. "Well, you'll have fun with Adelaide today," her mother said.

Hazel sighed. She used to play with Adelaide when they were little. There were pictures of the two of them splashing around the Linden Hills kiddie pool in matching arm floaties. But the Briggses left the country for four years, and when they came back neither girl wore floaties anymore. Adelaide liked making bead jewelry and putting nail polish on dolls. Hazel was into pirates. There was no compromise to be had.

"I haven't seen her in two years," Hazel said.

"Give her a chance, Hazel."

Hazel looked at the dashboard. Her mom didn't understand. She was perfectly willing to give everyone and everything a chance. It's just no one wanted to give her one.

They drove over to the Briggses' house slowly. The snow had stopped falling, but cars still inched carefully along the unplowed streets. Hazel's mom drove their car like it was an emotionally unstable bear.

The Briggses lived far from the blocks made up of rows of single-story houses plopped on top of place-mat yards where Hazel lived. There was nothing uneasy about the houses along this drive. They wore their second and third stories with assurance. No one had to dream up shutters and window boxes and trim, or porches and turrets and wide curving staircases. The snow covered the houses here, too—but where in Hazel's neighborhood it let the ordinary borrow magic from it, these houses seemed to be lending their power to the snow.

The Briggses lived on one of the lakes that lay in the heart of the city like a chain of jewels. There was an ice rink on it, complete with hockey boards and lights and a warming house, and as Hazel peered out her car window she saw families in matched sets sailing around the rink. She must have been the only girl in all of Minneapolis who did not know how to skate.

The Briggses' house perched on top of a small hill across from the lake, its red brick glowing against the white snow. It looked the size of Hazel's house and Jack's and one or two more put together. It made Hazel's look like a toy built from a cheap kit.

"Ready?" asked her mother as they parked.

"Sure," said Hazel.

The big dark-wood front door had an iron knocker on

it, the kind you'd expect Dracula to have, and Hazel tried to reach up for it. Her mom rested a hand on her shoulder. "It's just decoration," she whispered, pressing the doorbell.

And then Adelaide's mother was opening the door, and she smiled at Hazel, and Hazel was struck by how easy a thing it seemed for her to do. "Hazel!" she said. "You're all grown up! Come on in. Adie will be so happy to see you!"

Hazel took a breath before she entered, because it seemed like the sort of thing you should do. Inside, the house was all color and brightness and matching sets, the kind that had furniture that was just for decoration. And the smell . . .

"Elizabeth?" her mother asked. "Are you making . . . cookies?"

"Not me," Adelaide's mom said. She led them into the kitchen where Adelaide sat at a table, tapping a pencil against a notebook.

Hazel hadn't seen Adelaide in two years. Her dark hair had curled up and now hung around her face in tantalizing sproings. She had magenta horn-rimmed glasses that were probably very cool, though Hazel was no arbiter of such things. The kitchen around her, which was as big as Hazel's living room, looked like the sort of kitchen you see on TV, all matching and gleamy. Like Adelaide.

"Hi," Hazel said.

"Hi!" Adelaide said, gleaming. "I was just doing math

homework." She motioned to the textbook in front of her. "I've got so much."

"Oh," said Hazel. She looked down at Adelaide's textbook. She didn't recognize it. It struck her that she didn't know where Adelaide went to school, and if it was the sort of place that told you you had a good imagination or the sort of place that told you you needed to work on following the rules. "I probably can't help you."

"That's okay," Adelaide said, leaning in like she was telling a secret. "I can't help me either."

"I don't want to keep you," Hazel said, shifting.

"Oh, don't be a goof." Adelaide shut the book. "Come on, sit down."

Goof. Hazel blinked. "Okay." She crossed the kitchen and sat down on the cushioned oak chair next to Adelaide.

"What, I'm not here?" a male voice said.

Hazel turned. Adelaide's kitchen was big enough that if there was a man taking cookies out of the oven you might not immediately notice. Which in this case there was.

The man smiled at Hazel. He was roughly parent age and tall, with a poof of brown hair and sparkly gray eyes. He looked like the sort of person who might hand you an invitation to wizard school. "I'm Adelaide's uncle. You can call me Martin."

Hazel could not take it all in, the kitchen, the gleaming,

the uncle in the apron. This was the universe that everyone else lived in. She wanted to ask Adelaide to explain this place to her, to explain the rules, to show her the potion you had to drink to fit in here, but all she could say was "Your uncle makes cookies."

He shrugged. "They're from a tube."

"Uncle Martin's a screenwriter," Adelaide said. "That means he writes movies. But he can't sell them, so he's freeloading on my parents."

"That's right," her uncle said cheerfully. "But I make excellent tube cookies. I think it more than makes up for any freeloading."

"We're writing a story together," Adelaide told Hazel, eyes serious.

"Yes," said Uncle Martin. "Adie is going to make it up and then I am going to steal it and sell it for a jillion dollars and then who will be freeloading upon whom? But I will certainly put her name in the end credits. And yours, Ms. . . . ?

"Um . . . Hazel."

"What a lovely name," he said, nodding appreciatively. "Very heroic."

"Really?" Hazel said.

He turned to Adelaide. "Isn't that Lee Scoresby's dæmon's name?"

"No, that's Hester!" Adelaide looked at Hazel. "Have you read *The Golden Compass*?"

Like a thousand times. "Yeah," said Hazel.

"What do you think your dæmon would be?"

Hazel paused a moment, as if she hadn't already thought about this very carefully. "A cat," she said, because that was a normal thing to say.

"Really? I think it would be, like, an owl."

"Really?" Hazel asked.

"Mine is a slug," said Uncle Martin. "Now, Hazel, tell me your life story, from the beginning until you met me."

"Hazel's adopted," offered Adelaide. "From India."

Hazel blinked again, and looked from Adelaide to her wizard-school slug-dæmon uncle. It wasn't the sort of thing people usually came out and said.

"Really!" Martin said. "I want to go there someday off my screenwriting riches. Do you remember it at all?"

Hazel bit her lip. She supposed this was the sort of thing people with decorative furniture did. They just said things, because their houses had enough room for all kinds of things, no matter how odd and funny-shaped they were.

"No," she said. "I was just a baby."

"You should go back when you're older. It could be a quest, heroic Hazel." He nodded at her. "Now, Adie, tell Hazel the story I'm going to steal."

Adelaide nodded, her curls springing a little. "Okay," she said, leaning against the table toward Hazel. "There's a witch who lives wherever it's winter."

"We're starting with the villain," Martin interjected. "Because they are the most fun. Do you want to help, Hazel?"

She did. Adelaide looked at her expectantly. "The witch travels on a sleigh pulled by huge white wolves," Hazel began. This was not original. She tried again. "The wolves have mouths as red as blood. The snowflakes follow her like bees." She glanced at Adelaide, who nodded earnestly.

Uncle Martin smiled. "Like bees. Very evocative. Now, Adelaide, what does she wear?"

"A white dress and white furs," Adelaide said. "And she has a crown. Made of the thinnest of ice."

"Because she's a queen," Hazel said. "She's the Snow Queen."

"Yes, nice. Where does she live?"

"In a palace of ice," said Hazel. "And she has a heart to match."

"Very good." He looked at the two of them seriously. "And what does she want?"

Hazel and Adelaide exchanged a confused look. "What do you mean?" Adelaide asked.

"Everyone in a story wants something," he said.

"Especially the villains. And the hero's job is to stop them from getting it. So, what does she want?"

"Eternal winter?" said Adelaide.

"Kids," said Hazel. "She wants kids. She wants to collect them. She puts them in snow globes. She traps them with promises, and if she can get them to agree to stay there forever, they're hers."

The words came tumbling out of her mouth, and once they were out there she could only look from Martin to Adelaide in horror. This was the sort of thing she was not supposed to say out loud.

But Martin just turned to Hazel and nodded slowly. "Very good," he said. "You get a tube cookie. You, too, Adie."

"But . . . why?" Adelaide asked, looking from her uncle to Hazel. "The kids. Why would they agree to stay? Why would anyone stay with her?"

Martin stopped and regarded Hazel and Adelaide. "Yes," he said slowly. "Why. That's the question."

Hazel heard the sound of throat clearing. She had not noticed the two mothers step into the room. Her mom was looking at Adelaide's meaningfully, and Hazel knew that they had spent the last ten minutes talking about her. *See how she is?*

"Marty," Adelaide's mother warned, "you'll give them nightmares."

"Come on, Lizzie." He shook his head dismissively. "Kids can handle a lot more than you think they can. It's when they get to be grown up that you have to start worrying."

Adelaide smiled smugly at Hazel, and it was the sort of smile that invited her to smile smugly back. Which she did.

"So, did you have fun?" her mom asked as they drove off.

She did. "It was okay," Hazel said.

"We can go over to Adelaide's any time you want. I don't get to see Elizabeth much. It's nice for me. Maybe on the weekends?"

"Maybe," Hazel said. Weekends were for her and Jack. She needed to be there if he needed her.

They drove home on newly plowed streets, which their little car tackled eagerly. Hazel stared out of the window and watched the houses shrink and thought of villains and snow globes and what it would be like to be trapped inside.

When they pulled into the driveway, Hazel cast a glance over to Jack's house. It was dark. She wondered if he'd been able to make plans, if he was still out, or if he was home in his room, drawing or reading comic books or making up superhero baseball stats, with the shades drawn and the door closed. She wished he had a place to put all his funny-looking things.

Her heart panged. She was supposed to be with him, not eating tube cookies and speaking in fairy tales. She was his best friend. She would do better. Tomorrow.

Chapter Three

SPACES

The snow started up again just as Hazel was going to
sleep that night. It seemed innocuous, a soft coda to
the storm of the morning. There was no way to tell that
over the course of the night the sky would try to bury the
city.

Hazel woke up to her mother's knock on the door and
a gentle whisper, "You don't have to get up. School's canceled."

The sky did not bury the city, but it came close enough.
The street outside Hazel's house looked like it might only
be traversable by tauntaun. "Eighteen inches overnight,"
her mom told her when she came down for breakfast. "I've
never seen it come down like that. I hope there was nothing

you were dying to do at school today."

Hazel knew her mother really meant *I hope there is something you were dying to do at school today, that you are learning to love it there, and if you are not learning to love it there, can you please try harder?* Because her mom seemed to think it was the sort of thing Hazel could choose to do, like she could choose to understand the rules when they weren't even written in her language, like she could choose to make herself fit when she was so clearly shaped all wrong. She shrugged.

"Are you going to be okay by yourself?" her mom added, nodding toward her desk. "I've got—"

"Sure," Hazel said. "I'll go over to Jack's."

Her mother tilted her head. "Haze," she said slowly, "maybe it's better if Jack comes over here? Maybe you guys shouldn't—"

"Oh." Hazel shifted. "I think we're going sledding."

"Okay, good. And can you shovel the driveway for me today?"

"Sure."

"Thanks. Hey, um"—she leaned in to Hazel—"how's Jack doing these days? With everything."

"Okay, I think."

"Okay."

After breakfast, Hazel got on her boots and stepped

outside. The snow was almost up to her knees, and she had to lift her legs up to move through it, first one then the other—like she was trying to walk through butter.

There were no footprints outside of Jack's house. No one had tried to venture out yet. Hazel picked her way to the Campbells' front doorstep and rang their bell twice, their special ring. And waited. And waited. Just when she decided everyone must have slept in, the door opened. "Jack!" Hazel said, or was about to say when the word evaporated from her mouth. Standing in the doorway was someone she was not expecting to see at all: Jack's mom.

"Hello, Hazel," Mrs. Campbell said.

"Oh," said Hazel, shifting. "Hi."

It had been several weeks since Hazel had even laid eyes on Mrs. Campbell. She was wearing the same light-blue tee shirt and black yoga pants that she'd been in the last time Hazel saw her, but they were now faded and frayed. She was much thinner now, and surrounded by shadows. Her eyes were all wrong. They were like the eyes of the animals at the natural history museum, who were hollowed out and stuffed and posed and placed in some habitat and made to look like they were still alive. "You want Jack."

"Yes. Please," said Hazel.

"He was getting dressed. My husband's in the shower."

"Okay," said Hazel.

Mrs. Campbell blinked down at her. "It's nice to see you, Hazel," she said, and she stretched her face into a smile that held nothing. She looked like someone had severed her dæmon.

And then Jack appeared in the doorway next to her. "Mom, what are you doing?" He looked from her to Hazel. Hazel looked at the ground.

"The doorbell rang."

"I know, but . . . you should go sit down."

There was something about Jack, something subdued about his very appearance, as if he had dampened his own hue so as not to contrast with his mother's too brightly.

"Okay." She nodded at Jack and faded off.

"Let me get my stuff," Jack muttered. "Wait there."

There had been a time, not so long ago, when Jack had had a mom and Hazel had had a dad—that is, a real mom, the sort who did things besides sit in a beat-up easy chair and watch twenty-four-hour news networks and stare blankly at the world, and a real dad, the sort who lived with you or at least came to see you once in a while. Then one day Hazel did not have a dad anymore, because hers had left. And a couple days after that Jack had showed up on her doorstep and handed her his most prized possession, a baseball signed by Joe Mauer. Hazel had stared at it as if he'd just handed her his still-beating heart. "You should keep it," he had said.

"But . . . why?"

And he'd looked at her, almost bewildered, then said, "It's a Joe Mauer signed baseball," as if that was all that needed to be said. So Hazel took it, and she kept it on her bookshelf, and sometimes she looked at it and said to herself, *That is a Joe Mauer signed baseball*, and she understood.

Then one day Hazel went over to Jack's house to find his mom in the easy chair, except she wasn't there at all. It was like someone had snuck into their house in the middle of the night and stolen his mother. Except they'd forgotten to take her body.

And it wasn't too long after that that Hazel's mother sat her down and explained that Jack's mom was sad, that she was sick with sadness. And she asked if Hazel understood and Hazel said yes, though she didn't really.

"Why?" Hazel had asked.

"I don't know," her mother answered. "Sometimes there's no why."

Like an enchantment, Hazel thought. But at that moment she knew that it was not the thing to say out loud, and besides she could tell from her mother's voice that it was nothing like an enchantment, not at all.

And Jack's mother stayed sick with sadness, and her

eyes were so dead, and it was like she didn't see Jack, even when he was in front of her. And Hazel did not have anything for him, anything that was like her beating heart. And Jack never said a word about it, but sometimes he banged around and slammed doors, like he wanted to make sure he could still make noise, and sometimes he just kind of stopped, and it was like he had been frozen.

Now he stepped out of the house in his jacket and mittens, carrying his messenger bag, and closed the door firmly behind him.

"Sorry 'bout that," he said with a shrug.

Hazel got the urge to apologize back, but she did not know what for. "Are we gonna go sledding?"

Jack shrugged. "Let's go to the shrieking shack," he said. "I'll show you my new stuff."

The shrieking shack was an old skeleton of a house tucked away in a field near the railroad tracks. Jack had found it last summer, and he'd presented it to her like it was a palace. And it might as well have been, because it was all theirs.

Well, not all theirs. People came and they left trash behind and cigarette butts and beer bottles. They wrote things on the walls—tiny secret things in ballpoint pen and sprawling screaming things in spray paint. Hazel didn't mind. Because the people who left their secrets on the walls thought that this was some ordinary place, something for garbage and graffiti. Which meant that no one else had discovered that it was a palace in disguise.

It was winter and the sky had just tried to bury the city and this was not the time to go hang out in crumbling deserted houses, but—

"Okay," Hazel said.

It was a long journey through the snow today, down a couple of neighborhood blocks, then around the funny lime-green house with the tiny white fence, down the hill to the railroad tracks. The field was an ocean of snow that needed to be crossed—but there were no other footprints in it. It was all theirs.

The shack seemed to be waiting for them. The snow had ingratiated itself with the ruins of walls and memory of a roof, and it made it seem like the small dark-brown house had sprung out of the snow itself.

There would be a time when it wouldn't be safe for them to sit up in the small attic of the house anymore. The roof above them was falling in, the floor below them had places where it had rotted completely away. The house was decaying around them. But, for now, it was safe.

Hazel and Jack crossed through the empty doorway into the rotting shell of the first floor and trod gently up the stairs, stepping over the ones that had already given themselves to the rot.

There was a big enough hole in the roof for the winter sky to shine though, showing a dappling of snow on the wooden floor. It didn't matter—Hazel's jeans could not be wetter than they already were. She sat at their usual spot by the hole, which was just low enough in the slanted roof that you could sit on the floor and see the world outside. Jack settled in next to her.

There were some days, ever since the summer, when the whole feel of Jack seemed to change. Like suddenly, instead of being made of baseball and castles and super-heroes and Jack-ness, he was made of something scratchy and thick. Hazel could tell, because he had been her best friend for four years, and you can tell when your best friend is suddenly made of something else. And all she could do was try to remind him what he was really made of.

"So," she said. "Let me see what you got."

"Cool," Jack said. He opened up his bag and took out the sketchbook and began to flip through it. She watched the pages go by, thinking what a thing it must be to be good at something. There were figures and faces, some human, some monstrous, and they had some kind of life and light-ness to them, like the person who had drawn them could give them breath if he chose.

"What's that?" Hazel said. The last drawing was

something she hadn't seen before, something very different from everything else in the book.

"Oh. Nothing. I just drew it last night."

"Can I see?"

"Sure." Jack handed her the sketchbook. "It's not really anything."

Hazel looked at the page. This was a small sketch of a very simple palace—just a square, really, with four thin turrets coming up from each corner. Its edges were rounded a little bit, like it was made of clay or something. But it wasn't just the palace—he'd drawn a line under it across the paper to signify some kind of landscape. And the drawing of the palace was so small against the landscape, just a gesture in the middle of the page—like he had wanted to make it seem like it existed in the middle of infinite emptiness.

"You just don't usually do places."

"It's like a fort. It just kind of appeared there one day in the middle of the snow. And no one knows what it's for or how it got there. But if you're inside, no one can ever find you there."

"Oh," said Hazel, regarding the drawing carefully. In her head she began to imagine the story that would go with that place. "But who would want that?"

"There's a boy," Jack said. "He's just a normal boy. Until one day he wakes up and no one can see him. He's turned invisible. And he tries everything, but nothing works. So he goes here."

"Okay," said Hazel. She'd read a book once about a girl who turned invisible and a boy who could fly. Hazel knew she would be the invisible one, because she never got to be the one who flew. "Why does he go there?"

"Because it doesn't matter that he's invisible, you know? There's no one to look at him, and no one will ever come."

"Okay," Hazel said. "So, show me your bad guy."

Jack nodded and flipped back a couple of pages. The drawing was of what seemed to be an ordinary man, with a swath of thick black hair. Jack's heroes were usually muscular, but this one was tall and very thin and wearing an actual suit and tie, like someone you might run into downtown. It was his face where you could see there was something off—the shadows in his cheeks, like he lived on something other than food. And his eyes. Jack had spent a lot of time on his eyes. Hazel could see the life in them, she could see the intelligence behind them, and she knew if you found yourself gazing at these eyes very bad things were going to happen.

"Creepy," she said.

"I know!" Jack said. "He takes people's souls. Like a Dementor. But he's not just a monster, he's a supervillain. He's a genius."

"What does he want?" asked Hazel, thinking of Uncle Martin.

"Nothing." Jack said. "He's just bad for the sake of being bad. That's the scariest kind of villain, you know?"

Hazel nodded.

"And no one can fight against him," Jack continued. "Because what do you do against the guy who takes your soul? There's no superpower for that."

"But," said Hazel, feeling all of a sudden the dampness around her. "There's got to be something."

Jack studied his drawing carefully. "But what if there's not? What if no one can fight him?"

Hazel shrugged. She didn't know the answer. But there had to be a way. There was always a way.

Hazel and Jack spent the rest of the day sitting in the second floor of their house talking about supervillains and the secrets in their villain-y hearts. Jack had brought little packages of sandwich crackers and fruit snacks. This was the sort of thing he usually had now that his dad did all the shopping. Then it got to be time to go home, and the two trudged carefully back through the field. They were about to head up the hill that would take them back into the neighborhood, back into the ordinary world, when Hazel stopped.

"What is it?" asked Jack.

"I don't know," said Hazel. She turned back and regarded the decaying shell of the house for a moment. "I just wanted to look at it again." Then she shrugged and turned around to head back home.

When Hazel walked into her house, she found herself feeling scratchy and thick. As she wiped her feet in the vestibule, she heard her mom on the phone. Her voice sounded like it had no air in it, so Hazel knew who she was talking to. Hazel quietly got her boots and jacket off as she heard her mother's voice say, ". . . she just got in. Do you want to—" and then, a few moments later, her good-bye. Hazel lined up her boots against the wall and tucked her mittens and hat into her jacket.

"Did you have fun sledding?" her mom asked as she came in.

"Yeah," said Hazel, hanging her jacket in the front closet.

"Hey, listen. Elizabeth Briggs called. Adelaide was hoping you might come over on Saturday morning."

"I have plans," Hazel said.

Her mother leaned back in her chair and looked at Hazel. "I already accepted," she said. "Hazel, honey, it's not wrong to make other friends. You'd still be a wonderful friend to Jack."

Hazel rubbed the floor with her stockinged foot. "Whatever," she muttered, and went into her room and closed the door to go read for the rest of the night. Some things you just couldn't fight against.

When Hazel woke up the next morning, she found the scratchy feeling had not gone away. It didn't help when she looked out of her window to find her street had been plowed perfectly. There was no snow day today.

Her mom was cranky at breakfast and gave Hazel a talking-to about snow shoveling and maturity and accepting responsibility. And Hazel could not explain that she had forgotten, that there was Jack and soul-sucking villains, and sometimes you are too scratchy to remember the things you are supposed to do, even if you do feel really bad about it later.

It was snowing when she went to the bus stop, the sort of snow that feels like sharp little ice pellets on your skin. They hurt Hazel's face. And Jack wasn't there, and she hated when he wasn't where he was supposed to be. It was terrible when people weren't at the places they were supposed to be. Jack didn't get to the bus stop until just as they were loading, and then he was immediately called over by Tyler and Hazel was left to sit by herself and she'd forgotten her book.

She walked into school behind everyone and stopped in the bathroom, but still when she peered into Mr. Williams's classroom window Jack wasn't sitting down yet, and his empty desk nudged at her like something important that's just out of the reach of memory. She was thinking about something else in the hallway and didn't see Bobby taking off his boots and accidentally kicked him in the thigh. Bobby yelped and clutched his leg and told her that in addition to being crazy she was a stupid klutz cow.

Mrs. Jacobs read announcements that morning. Remember to bang the snow off your boots when you come into school, field trip to the art museum next week and ask your parents if they'll chaperone, remember no peanuts for the bake sale, and, oh, Mikaela and her dad are going to start a father-daughter book club if anyone's interested.

And then, from behind her:

"Wow, Hazy, that sounds like fun. Too bad your dad isn't around!"

Hazel whirled around. Bobby was snickering. Mikaela sucked in her breath. Even Tyler shook his head. Bobby rolled his eyes in response.

Hazel turned back around and focused on a small spot at the front of her desk and did not lift her eyes.

At recess, Jack was waiting for her again by the big slide, and he looked at Hazel like he had no idea how scratchy she was. She always knew when he was scratchy, always. Bobby called to him, and he lifted his hand to wave.

Hazel's eyes narrowed. "How can you be friends with them?" she asked.

Jack blinked. "What do you mean?"

She lifted her hand to wipe snow from her forehead. "Bobby and Tyler. They're jerks. They're mean to me. I'm your best friend."

"Whatever! They're idiots, Hazel. You shouldn't listen to them."

"But you're friends with them."

Jack just stared at her, like he did not see the contradiction, like he could not even fathom what it was.

"Why don't you just go hang out with them today then," Hazel said, crossing her arms.

"What's with you?"

"Nothing."

"Okay, fine," Jack said, looking at her like she had a mental disorder. He stared at her a moment, and then turned to walk toward the boys.

Hazel stood, the pelletlike snow falling around her, and then, so quickly it was like she had superpowers, she bent down and packed a snowball and hurled it at him.

It hit his back. He whirled around. "What the—"

And then it was Hazel's turn to walk away, leaving Jack

standing there in the snow.

It took three steps for the remorse to hit her. One. Two. Three. She stopped. She was about to turn around, to open her mouth and see if any of the right words would come out, when she heard a yelp from Jack. She turned. He was bent over, clutching his left eye. "Ow!" he yelled. "Ow!" His voice cracked into the sky. His other hand flew to his chest, and he fell to his knees. Mrs. Jacobs and Mr. Williams were there next to him in a flash.

"What is it? What happened?"

But Jack just gargled something into the air and rocked back and forth, clutching his eye.

A crowd gathered around him as the teachers looked at each other, bewildered. Hazel stared, helplessly, as Mr. Williams lifted Jack up onto his feet and began to help him inside while Jack clutched at his face and groaned. Hazel started to follow, but Mrs. Jacobs stopped her. And so she stood and watched as Mr. Williams led Jack away, because there was nothing at all she could do.

Chapter Four

PIECES

In a flash, the fifth graders of Lovelace Elementary were crowded around Hazel.

"What happened?"

"Did his eye fall out?"

"Is he going to be blind?"

It was the first time they'd ever wanted to hear what she had to say. But for once she had no story to tell.

There are things you do not notice until they are gone. Like the certainty that your body is a single whole, that there's something keeping you from breaking into pieces and scattering with the winds. Now Hazel could feel pieces of her threatening to break off, and she was no longer sure her feet would stay attached to the ground.

Jack was hurt. She felt it as if it had happened to her. She would have preferred that it had happened to her, because then she wouldn't be standing here, helpless, with the entire fifth grade looking to her. Hazel could fight anything—dragons, wicked witches, evil baseball-playing supervillains, but she needed Jack beside her. He was supposed to be beside her.

She looked around at the other kids. The girls huddled up, whispering and pointing. The boys shuffled around and did not look anyone in the eye.

Except for two of them. Bobby and Tyler were both shooting her nasty looks. Hazel met their eyes and scowled at them. They scowled back.

Mrs. Jacobs put her hand on Hazel's back and whispered, "He'll be all right."

Hazel turned to look up at her teacher, trying to discern whether she meant *I have actual knowledge that I am imparting to you about Jack's condition* or *I have no idea whether he'll be okay but since I am a grown-up I think pretending I do is somehow comforting to you.*

Then the bell rang, and Mrs. Jacobs motioned everyone into the building. Hazel looked at the spot where Jack had been, but there was nothing there except the impression his legs left in the snow.

❄

Nobody could sit still in Mrs. Jacobs's class that afternoon, least of all Hazel. Her desk was positioned just so she could almost see out the door. Almost. When Mrs. Jacobs wrote on the blackboard, Hazel would lean forward, trying to catch some glimpse of Jack-like movement in the hallway. This time, it would be him peeking in the doorway, Hazel making some kind of face, and in that face she would say, *I'm so glad you are back* and *I hope you're okay* and *I'm so so sorry.* And he would be able to read all of it.

It was just something in his eye, she tried to tell herself. Maybe he would need an eye patch. He would like that. Jack knew the value of an eye patch.

But Hazel had had things stuck in her eye before, and it did not make her want to rip her face off. And Jack—Jack never felt a thing. That's what he said whenever he hurt himself: "I never feel a thing." It was one of his powers, he said. She had never seen anything hurt anyone the way this hurt Jack.

It was just something in his eye.

She could not get the image out of her head of the impression of his legs in the snow. And anyone else who looked wouldn't understand; they would just see two leg-size trenches and wonder what had made them. They would just think that this was an empty thing, that that's what's supposed to be, that there's something perfectly normal about a thing that exists entirely because it is lacking something.

"Hazel," snapped Mrs. Jacobs. "Pay attention!"

Hazel turned back around and slumped in her seat. She should have followed Jack. Why did she let Mrs. Jacobs stop her? They'd traveled through earth's molten core, the Arctic, through space and beyond together, and she'd let a fifth-grade teacher with no imagination stop her? Maybe it was all a conspiracy, maybe they had done something to him, poisoned him somehow, maybe he was being held captive somewhere, maybe he needed her to rescue him—

A folded-up note landed on Hazel's lap. Her name was written on the front in boyish print. She unfolded it and beheld the words *It's your fault.*

Hazel turned in her seat and glared at the boys in the back. Tyler mouthed *your fault*. Bobby glared at her. "Crazy Hazy," he hissed.

In one motion Hazel stood up, grabbed the hard pencil case from her desk, and hurled it at Tyler. There were some yelps, some gasps, and then absolute quiet. Even Mrs. Jacobs had been shocked into stillness.

The pencil case ricocheted off Tyler's face and clattered on the desk. Pencils rolled everywhere. They were the only movement in the room. Hazel stood there, looking at the frozen tableau of her class, at the shocked faces of the other kids, at Tyler who was clutching his face, at Mrs. Jacobs who seemed to have short-circuited, and decided she was not sorry. Not in the least bit. She gave the room one last look, turned, and stomped out.

She looked into Mr. Williams's room to see Jack's desk was still empty. Mr. Williams had returned, though. Hazel could not believe he had not stopped into her classroom to give them an update. Hazel wanted to run in and ask him, but the sound of clanky footsteps from the room behind her indicated Mrs. Jacobs had regained function, so Hazel sprung off on her heel and ran down three flights of stairs into the girls' locker room, where a bunch of surprised-looking fourth graders were changing into their gym clothes. Hazel straightened purposefully and gave them the sort of look fifth graders give fourth graders to keep them in line, then walked into one of the bathroom stalls and curled up in a ball on the toilet, where she sat until the end of the school day. And if anyone saw her, they would think that this was the way she was supposed to be, that it was perfectly normal to be a thing created out of the lack of something else.

Finally the school bell rang, and Hazel unballed herself from the toilet and opened the stall. Her legs groaned as if they would have liked nothing more than to be curled up like that forever.

Everyone was streaming out of the school, and there

was no going back for her backpack or her jacket, because she did not need to add missing the bus to her list of crimes. And she didn't particularly want to face anyone in the class—never again, really. But certainly not now.

When you throw something at someone else, it's usually not a considered action. Hazel, really, had not thought things through. If Hazel had thought things through, she might have realized that elementary schools do not take kindly to students throwing things at other students, or to them stomping out of class, or to completely disappearing in the middle of the day. She might have realized that these activities would result in an inevitable call to her mother, and that her mother, too, would not take kindly to the throwing, stomping, or disappearing, and that when Hazel snuck out of a back door of the building at the end of the day without her backpack, jacket, hat, or mittens and walked around the whole school to head to the buses, her mother would, inevitably, be there waiting for her.

"What were you thinking? Where were you? What happened?" All these words came sputtering out of her mother's mouth at once, but Hazel got the drift.

"I'm sorry."

"You're sorry? You're sorry? Do you know how worried I was? You just disappear like that? We looked everywhere for you!"

Hazel's heart sank. "I'm sorry," she said again.

Her mother shook her head and grabbed her phone. "I have to call Mr. Yee," she said. "To let him know you haven't been kidnapped. Principals don't really like it when fifth graders disappear in the middle of the day."

As Hazel's insides churned, her mom talked on the phone to the principal. She said "uh-huh" a lot and "I see" and "Yes, I'll take care of it," and Hazel got the distinct feeling that that "it" was she. Her mom hung up, and turning to Hazel, started to put it away.

"Wait. Can we call Jack?" The words burst out of Hazel's mouth.

"What?" This was not one of those *whats* that was asking *What did you say?* Or *Could you delve deeper so I could better understand your meaning?*

"He was hurt. Something hurt him. Something got in his eye. He was hurt really bad and they took him away and I don't know what happened because I didn't follow him and I threw a snowball." Tears pricked in Hazel's eyes.

Her mother's expression softened. "Oh. Is that what this is about?"

Hazel nodded.

"Oh, honey." Her mother sighed. "I'm sorry he got hurt. I really am. That must have been really hard. But . . . he got something in his eye. Is that really worth all this drama?"

Hazel's cheeks went red. It wasn't just that. She couldn't quite say what it *was*, though.

Her mom sighed and rubbed her forehead. "You're getting older now, and I think it's time to control your imagination a little bit. Because it causes you to act in ways that are not always appropriate. Like throwing things at people."

Hazel blushed. It wasn't like she would throw things at just anyone.

"You could have hurt Tyler, you know. And no matter how upset you are, that's just not okay, do you understand?"

Hazel shrugged. She heard Bobby's voice in her head and wondered why it was she who was not allowed to hurt anyone.

"You have to live in reality sometimes," her mother continued. "Even when it's not fun. And reality is that you go to Lovelace now. This is a different school, and you have to behave a certain way. The reality is that sometimes people we love get hurt and we can't just turn into the Incredible Hulk. "

Hazel looked at the floor. The Incredible Hulk batted .273 with a slugging percentage of .581. He was a disaster in the field, though.

Her mom shook her head and exhaled. The car was quiet, suddenly, and the air was scratchy and thick. "I know it's hard with your dad gone," she said finally. "It's hard for me, too. And I'm trying the best I can. But"—she turned to Hazel—"we need to work together. I can't do this alone. I can't come running to school because you're missing. I can't be getting emails from your teacher all the time about your behavior. Part of being grown up is acting the way you're supposed to act, even if you don't feel like it. Can you be grown up for me?"

Hazel understood. Being grown up meant doing what grown-ups wanted you to do. It meant sacrificing your imagination for rules. It meant sitting quietly in your desk chair while your best friend is helicoptered off for emergency eye surgery. It meant letting people say whatever they wanted to you.

But her mother seemed so tired, and so sad, and it wasn't like Hazel tried to make trouble. She wanted to do well in school and make friends and have her teachers like her and have her mom be happy and proud of her. She just didn't seem to know how.

"I'll try," she said quietly.

"Good," said her mom. "Now, Mr. Yee told me that some things are going to happen at school. You're going to meet with the counselor. We're going to go for evaluations."

"Mrs. Jacobs hates me."

"She doesn't hate you, Hazel. You have to see things from her perspective. She's got a big class to manage. She's just trying to do her job, honey. You never know what some-one else is going through, right?"

Hazel shrugged.

"Everyone just wants to help you," her mother said.

Hazel stared at the dashboard. Up until this year, nobody thought she needed help.

"It will be okay. You've been through a lot, and everyone needs help sometimes. That's all." She touched Hazel gen-tly on the shoulder. "Now. Let's call over to Jack's and see what's going on."

So Hazel's mother called up Jack's home, while Hazel leaned in to listen. It is not an easy thing, to keep yourself from exploding. She could hear the drone of Jack's dad's voice from the receiver but couldn't make out any words. She tugged at her mom's coat and whispered, "Let me talk to Jack," once, and then again. Her mom nodded, and an eternity later she said, "Oh, all right then," and "I'll let her know," and "Thank you very much, Kevin," and then, "Is Jack available to talk?" and finally she stopped talking, and as Hazel reached for the phone, she hung up.

Hazel gaped at her mother.

"He couldn't talk," she said, starting the car. "He was busy."

"Busy? Busy doing *what*?"

"I don't know. But he's okay. He got glass in his eye."

"Glass?" Hazel imagined a shard of glass the size of a small knife sticking out of Jack's eye.

"Yeah. They can't imagine how it happened. There must have been some in the snow, and . . ." Her eyes traveled to Hazel and then snapped back. "But it wasn't very much, and they got it out."

"But . . . it really hurt him!"

"He's okay now, honey. That's what matters. It wasn't a big deal."

Hazel flushed. "It looked like a big deal!"

"I know. I know."

"Can we go over there?"

Her mother frowned. "I don't know. Mr. Campbell said he was busy."

"He's not too busy to see me." Hazel folded her arms and slumped in her seat. Jack was never "busy." He would never *not* want to talk to her. They were keeping something from her. Something was wrong.

Of course her mother had to stop at the grocery store on the way home, because it was completely grown up to be worried about how much cereal there was in the house instead of a boy with a glass knife in his eye. Hazel sat in the front seat while her mom spent a lifetime in the grocery store, barely resisting the urge to punch through the window. It would accomplish nothing but maybe get glass in her eye, but then at least she might know what Jack was going through.

Hazel burst out of the car when they got home and ran to Jack's front door before her mother could stop her. She still didn't have her jacket. She stood on the doorstep, afraid for a moment to knock, because something was up, something was wrong, because they wouldn't let her talk to him, because she'd let Jack be led off.

But whatever it was, Jack needed her. Now was not the time to stand on doorsteps, heart pounding; it was time to stride through the door and see what awaited on the other side.

So she rang the doorbell. Twice, because that was their signal.

Jack's mom opened the door.

"Oh," said Hazel, again. "Hi."

"Hello," said Mrs. Campbell, who seemed like she might fall over with the effort of it. "Where's your jacket?"

Hazel blinked. "I'm . . . fine, Mrs. Campbell." She peered into the house. "Is Jack here?"

"Oh, sure," Mrs. Campbell said, smiling that half-smile she had now, a smile that existed because it was lacking something.

Footsteps, then—a herd of them, as if Jack's accident

had caused him to duplicate. And at first Hazel thought he had, because three boys appeared in front of her where she had been expecting one. Hazel stared. Jack was fine, no eye patch, no shard of glass sticking out of his eye, no permanent disfigurement. Bobby and Tyler surrounded him like guards.

"Oh," Hazel said.

"Oh, hi, *Hazel*," said Bobby.

Tyler glared and made a show of rubbing the spot on his head where the pencil case had hit him.

Hazel ignored them. "I called you," she said to Jack. "To see how you were. Your dad said you were busy."

"Bobby and Tyler were coming over," Jack said, shrugging.

"I wanted to see how you were," she repeated. So the boys had come over after school to see how he was, and she, his best friend, had sat in the car at the grocery-store parking lot and did not punch through the window. "I'm sorry. But I tried calling and your dad said—"

"Yeah. I was busy."

"Are we going outside, or what?" Bobby asked the other boys. Jack started bouncing up and down on his feet.

Hazel blinked. "Um," she said, looking at Jack. "I think I figured out about the soul-sucker. Someone has to have a power, just like a blocking power. And at first that seems really useless, really small when you consider all the powers in the world. But then it turns out they're the only one who can stop this guy . . ."

Bobby snickered. Tyler snorted. And Jack ran a hand through his brown hair and shook his head.

"Oh, Hazel," he said, "stop being such a baby."

"Come on," said Bobby. "We gotta go!"

"Yeah, let's go," Jack said. "We'll go out the back." And with that they disappeared into the house, leaving Hazel standing in the front hall, alone.

Chapter Five

THE MIRROR

Now, the world is more than it seems to be. You know this, of course, because you read stories. You understand that there is the surface and then there are all the things that glimmer and shift underneath it. And you know that not everyone believes in those things, that there are people—a great many people—who believe the world cannot be any more than what they can see with their eyes.

But we know better.

So we are going to leave Hazel for a moment and step into the glimmering, shifting world. Because there is something there you need to see.

Or rather, someone.

We'll call him Mal, though that is not his real name.

His real name has forty-seven syllables, and we have things to do.

Mal looks like nothing you know or can imagine, neither goblin nor troll nor imp nor demon. But neither the goblins nor the trolls nor the imps nor even the demons know what Mal is either. For Mal is not any one of those things, but all of them.

Mal is a goblin. He has green-brown skin, a froglike mouth, and sharp little teeth. Mal is a troll. He is seven feet tall and warty, has terrible breath, and a penchant for hanging out under bridges. Mal is an imp. He has small bat wings, a high-pitched screech of a laugh, and pointy little ears. Mal is a demon. And that means he is up to no good.

But we are not interested in Mal for who he is—and we'll be leaving him soon enough. We are interested in him for what he has done.

If you had encountered Mal just a few days before this story began, you would have found him in very good spirits. For Mal had just invented something delightful—or at least something that he found delightful, which is altogether a different prospect.

On the surface, it looked like an ordinary mirror. It was about the size of a tall man. It was oval shaped, like something you would find covered by a white sheet in an old haunted house. It had a thick frame carved with winged beings crawling and clamoring all over each other. The beings looked like angels at first. It was only when you got close enough that you could see that their faces were like skulls and their eyes were filled with menace.

There was nothing ordinary about that mirror. And if you were the perceptive sort—which of course you are—you would have known it immediately. But if you weren't, you might look in the mirror and think, *I did not know that mole was so enormous* or *Why is my face festering?* Or *My goodness, I had no idea I was so evil looking.* For the mirror took beautiful things and made them ugly, and it took ugly things and made them hideous.

It was most marvelous mischief indeed.

Mal took the mirror around, reflecting everything he could in it, delighting in the transformations he saw. A rose garden looked like piles of boiled spinach. A grove of trees became a charred wasteland. A sparkling lake turned into burbling oil.

And then he decided he would fly it up into the sky, right up to the heavens, to see the sparkling blue earth look like a mean shriveled-up thing.

So Mal took the mirror and flew into the sky. He flew up, up, up.

And something happened.

Something unexpected.

Something fateful.

Mal flew too high, and the mirror began to protest. The mirror creaked, then the mirror cracked.

It shattered into a hundred million pieces in Mal's hands. The pieces caught in the wind and landed all across the earth below. The beings of the hidden earth came out to watch.

And so did the witch.

She had come because of the snow. She could travel from one snowy world to another—to her it was all the same place. She liked heavy snowfalls the best, the kind that blankets the world in white quiet, the kind where the snowflakes are big enough to show their architecture, the kind that, if there is any magic to be had in the world, would make it come out.

She stayed in the woods where all the hidden creatures were, and the trees feared her. She moved through the shadows and kept her eye on the glimmering world outside. She felt the mirror shatter in the sky, she closed her eyes and saw its story spread back into the past, she fell with the tiny shards as they spread over the earth. Some fell to the ground. Some landed in trees, turning the bark black. And one, one landed in the eye of a boy, and she saw it as if she were right there.

"Oh," said the witch, placing a long finger on her cheek. "This should be interesting."

Chapter Six

CASTOFFS

Hazel walked in the front door of her house, trailing snow behind her. Her feet were soaked in their sneakers, and she was shivering underneath her thin shirt. She didn't really care.

Her mom was already at her desk in the living room doing work. She looked up as her daughter walked in.

"You don't have a jacket!" she exclaimed.

"I left it at school, remember?"

"Oh, Hazel." She shook her head. "You're shivering. Come in and get warm. Wasn't Jack home?"

Hazel looked at the ground. "He . . . he had Bobby and Tyler over." There. That was true.

"Oh," her mom said. It was an *Oh* with a question attached.

"Yeah," Hazel added quickly. "They were gonna go sledding and, you know"—she gestured to her jacketless body—"I don't have my stuff."

Her mother perked up. "Well, that was sensible of you, Haze. You're making good choices."

Hazel grimaced. In books a good choice is choosing to go fight the dragon. In Hazel's life, it's not going sledding because you left your boots at school.

And, of course, she hadn't made that choice at all. In real life you don't get to make choices. You're just not invited.

"Do you need the desk to do your homework?" her mother said, motioning in front of her.

"Um . . . " Even if she wanted to, Hazel could not do her homework because it was all still in her backpack in Mrs. Jacobs's room. It didn't matter. They were already going to send her to the school counselor. She was already a problem, she might as well start acting like it.

"No. I don't."

"Honey"—her mother tilted her head—"are you all right?"

Hazel shrugged. "Sure." She looked away so her mom wouldn't see the lie on her face, then excused herself and went into her room, closing the door behind her.

She lay down on the bed, moving her pile of stuffed

animals aside. She reached over to grab one of them, but Jack's words rang in her head. *Stop being such a baby.* Her hand retracted, and she wrapped her arms around her chest and hugged herself.

There was a Nithling in her stomach, chomping away at everything around it. Tears filled her eyes, and she squeezed them away. She was not a baby. She was Hazel, and Jack was her best friend. Why would he act like that?

In the back of her mind she heard Adelaide's uncle's voice: *Why? That's the question.*

There was a reason. People don't just change like that. Jack wouldn't be mean to her. He just wasn't himself. He could have been in shock, still. She would be in shock, too, if she'd gotten glass in her eye. Maybe they'd given him some medication that made him weird. That happened all the time. Or maybe he was trying to keep her out of his house, like there was some kind of secret there, something bad, and he was trying to keep her safe, and he was sorry he had to do it like that but he had to keep her out for her own protection and that was the only way to do it. He'd explain tomorrow. He'd explain and apologize. She just had to wait.

Hazel woke up the next morning and the monster in her stomach immediately chomped down. Everything clenched up, and two moments later she remembered why.

She went to her window to find that ice had covered the world. The street in front of her glimmered menacingly. Huge icicles hung down from the rows of houses like spikes. The trees looked as if they had been mummified. Ice coated Hazel's window, and she wondered if the whole house was encased in it. They would open the front door only to find a foot-thick wall blocking them from everything beyond it. They'd peer at the world beyond but would only be able to see blurs and splotches, and soon they would forget what it was like to see things for what they were.

Hazel looked over at Jack's house. She didn't know what she was expecting to see, maybe a banner hanging from the window reading

I'M SORRY, HAZEL. I DIDN'T MEAN IT.

That would have been the best thing.

But it wasn't there.

She left her room, feeling a little like she was crossing a moat—except the alligators were all inside her, snapping away.

She had breakfast, then her mom emerged from the basement holding something puffy and purple. "I found your old jacket. Good thing I didn't give it away yet."

Hazel stared. The jacket shone. "I can't wear that."

"Why not? I know it's small. It was small last year."

"It's too . . . " Hazel shook her head. *Babyish*, she thought.

"You loved this two years ago," her mom said with a little smile. "I can't let you freeze to death, honey. It's just for the morning."

Soon Hazel was dressed in her third-grade jacket. It went down to her mid-waist, and her wrists stuck out. She looked like a puffy purple pauper. Her mom then produced a hot pink hat with purple stars embroidered on it and sparkly silver strands in the puff on top, and hot pink mittens to match. Hazel could only dress herself slowly in her own brightly hued humiliation. She tried to put on the glittery boots her mother gave her but couldn't get her feet into them.

She looked up at her mom. Her mom closed her eyes. "All right," she said. "I'll drive you."

Even the half of her that was desperate to see Jack at the bus stop, to hear his explanation, to get as quickly as possible to the moment when everything was all right again, did not want to do so dressed like a spastic eight-year-old's birthday hat.

"Thanks, Mom," she muttered.

Hazel had always felt invisible when she walked into school alone, and she thought that that was the worst way you could possibly feel. That was before she'd turned into a walking purple and pink glitter marshmallow. All she could do was keep her head down and count the steps to the school, while her mother watched out the car window, not understanding that freezing to death would be better than this.

Just in front of the entrance to the school, her sneak-ered foot landed on a patch of ice. Her back slammed against the ground. Hazel lay there as elementary school students gathered around her, and it seemed that not even the third graders were dressed as ridiculously as she was.

Hazel slowly picked herself up and headed into the school, her body now feeling as beat up as her heart. As soon as she crossed through the front door, she shed herself of the accoutrements of her absurdity, and had to fight the urge to dump them behind a wastebasket. Her sneakers were soaked from the snow. Her jeans were wet from the encounter with the ice. She felt like slush.

She walked through the hallways alone. She had done this before, but there was always the idea of Jack, a ghost of him that grinned as it accompanied her.

She wondered if people could hear the pounding of her heart, if the monstrous thrumming caused the kindergart-ners in their classroom to look around wide-eyed with fear as she passed, if the before-school-care kids in the music room unwittingly began to shake their maracas in time with it, if soon the very walls of the building would shake with it.

She went up to Jack's classroom and peered through the window. He was there, just as he was supposed to be. She thought at him, as hard as she could. One moment. Two. Three.

Four. Five.

He did not turn around.

Hazel shrank backward.

She walked into her classroom, breathing ice. Someone mumbled, "Tyler, she's got a pencil case, duck!" and someone else cackled.

Hazel flinched. She'd forgotten that part. She crawled into her desk and began to fiddle with the backpack she'd left there the day before, while people whispered around her.

And then Mrs. Jacobs was standing over her. "Good morning, Hazel," she said, carefully articulating each word. And then she stopped and stood in silence. She said nothing else, nothing about the day before. An artificial smile spread across her face, and Hazel got the feeling she was supposed to congratulate the teacher on her generosity.

Hazel looked down and got out her notebook, and Mrs. Jacobs turned away. The bell rang and the teacher began to talk, and Hazel's brain identified her voice as background noise and moved it to the rear of her consciousness.

Hazel looked out the window, wondering how many cars she would watch pass by until recess when she saw Jack again.

What would he say to her? Would he try to explain? Or would he pretend it had never happened? Maybe he didn't even remember, maybe he'd been in so much shock that he had amnesia. That would explain a lot. Hazel would understand. She'd never even tell him how he'd acted, she'd keep it secret for the rest of her days.

Her eyes fell on the trees that lined the sidewalk. Ice had colonized them like alien goo. She wondered what they felt. Were they cold underneath all of that, chilled to the roots? Or did they feel safe now?

"Hazel!" snapped Mrs. Jacobs. "What do I have to do to get you to pay attention? You're supposed to be taking notes. Please get out a pencil. We'll wait for you."

Snickers, whispers, and the hum of impatience from Mrs. Jacobs.

"Psycho," hissed Bobby.

Hazel opened her desk. Her pencil box was nowhere to be found. Mrs. Jacobs cleared her throat.

"I don't have anything to write with," Hazel mumbled. Her skin felt like it was burning from the force of the thirty pairs of eyes fixed on her.

"I see," said Mrs. Jacobs. Her mouth tightened, and Hazel heard all of the things she was not saying. "Would someone loan Hazel a pencil, please?"

Hazel's skin seared. One moment. Two. Then, next to her, Mikaela leaned over. "Here you go," she said softly. She blinked and added, "I have highlighters, too, if you need them."

Hazel nodded, unable to speak.

Then, a hiss from behind her. "I don't know, Tyler, that looks pretty sharp!"

"Yeah. Be careful, man. Girls with pencils are pretty fierce."

Hazel whirled around in her seat to find Tyler's face had turned red and he was staring intently at the desk in front of him. And then she understood.

Jack was mad at her for throwing her pencil case at Tyler. It made sense; since she'd come to Lovelace he'd had to negotiate things with them delicately so he didn't hurt their feelings. Boys were very sensitive. And Jack did it, he did a really good job, he played with her at recess and sat with them on the bus. But then Hazel had to go and embarrass Tyler in front of the whole class. And that put Jack in a really bad position.

The ice inside her melted away. This she could fix. She

would apologize to Jack, and then everything would be okay again.

Hazel pressed her legs together and tried not to fidget in her chair. She was going to have to survive until recess when she could see Jack. She would apologize, and then she would tell him to go off and play football with the boys, so then everyone would feel better, especially Hazel, because it feels good to apologize, it feels good to do the right thing. Hazel was making good choices!

Hazel realized her fingers were beating a rapid rhythm on the desk. She covered the offending hand with her other one, took a deep breath, and forced herself to look at Mrs. Jacobs. The teacher had put images of what looked like crystal snowflake ornaments on the overhead projector.

"Do you see that every single one of them has the same number of sides?" she was saying. "Six, right? This is called—"

"Hexagonal symmetry!" The words burst out of Hazel's mouth.

Mrs. Jacobs blinked. "Very good, Hazel. 'Hexagon,' for 'six-sided,' and 'symmetry,' meaning the sides are exactly the same. A snowflake is mathematically perfect. In the media you'll see drawings of snowflakes that are eight sided, but you'll know that this is scientifically inaccurate." She smiled at the class as if she had given them a great gift. "Now, these photographs of snowflakes were taken by a scientist named Wilson Bentley over a hundred years ago. They called him 'Snowflake' Bentley, and he was the one who discovered that no two snowflakes were alike."

Mrs. Jacobs began to yammer on about the formation of snowflakes—supercooled droplets, layers of atmosphere, blah blah—which was the same information Hazel had ignored from her mother three days ago. Hazel impatiently drew some snowflakes on her notebook. She was careful to make them eight sided.

Finally, it was time for recess, and Hazel sprang out of her chair and gathered her things. Outside she darted over to the big slide to wait for Jack.

Mr. Williams's class emerged out the back door, and Hazel stood on her tiptoes scanning the faces. He wasn't there, and wasn't there, and then he was. Hazel's heart sped up, and it was all she could do to keep from jumping and waving.

Jack stopped and looked around. His eyes passed right over the big slide and Hazel and moved on, stopping at the edge of the fence. A grin spread across his face, and he ran toward the boys that congregated there.

Hazel squeezed her eyes shut. Of course he wouldn't come. It was only natural. He was still mad.

She was not afraid. She marched right over to the boys

who were huddled together laughing. She tapped Jack on the shoulder. He turned around and looked at her blankly.

"Jack," she said, straightening. "I'm sorry I threw a pencil box at Tyler. It put you in a bad position. I should have thought about you. I was a bad friend and I'm sorry."

There! Hazel smiled.

Jack raised his eyebrows and looked at Tyler. "She threw a pencil box at you?"

Tyler rolled his eyes. "Yup."

"*Psy*-cho," Bobby muttered under his breath.

Jack cocked his head at Hazel. "Why are you apologizing to *me*?"

"Oh," Hazel said. A tendril of something began to rise up in her stomach. "Right." She turned to look at Tyler. "Tyler, I'm sorry I threw a pencil case at you."

Tyler wrinkled up his nose. "All right," he said.

Hazel looked back at Jack. The tendril was at her heart now.

He shrugged at her. "Okay. Well, see ya, Hazel."

And then the boys ran off.

Hazel spent the rest of the day encased in ice. She did not talk to anyone, as you would expect from someone encased in ice. She looked out of the window and understood, now, how the trees felt. Not chilled, not safe, just somehow disconnected from everything.

Today was a bus day, and she took her seat early and glued her eyes out the window so she did not have to see Jack. She heard him, though, as he approached snickering with the other boys. There was a banging sound and the boys all laughed, and Jack's laughter was the loudest of all. She kept her eyes where they were, but her foolish heart still sped up thinking he might choose today to sit next to her.

He did not.

Hazel bit down hard on her lip and watched the world go by.

At school she was so good at looking out the window and tuning everything else out. She was a professional, she could teach a class. But not here. Here on the bus the raucous voices of the boys in back slapped against her like an angry sea. In the air around her, Jack laughed, Jack hooted, Jack cackled, Jack snickered, Jack was a whole thesaurus entry of glee, and Hazel could only let the waves batter her.

She had had no idea before that day how long the bus ride was, how slowly the driver moved through the streets. Every stop was a lifetime. The brakes creaked.

The stop sign on the side of the bus inched its way into place, struggling to push past the uncompromising air. The bus door opened with a hissing *psst*, like it was telling a secret. The first graders gathered their things, thing at a time, and stumbled by with their tiny little legs. Down the stairs. Out the door. In front of the bus. The blinkers ticked, perpetually. Onto the sidewalk. *Psst,* the door closed. The stop sign inched its way back, the bus trembled, then plodded down a block or two to do it all again.

Finally, they got to their block, and with a *creak, push, tick tick, psst,* it was time for Hazel to get off. She gathered her things with the precision and care of a first grader, but it did not matter. Jack burst through the aisle as if he'd been shot from a cannon and was off the bus and down the sidewalk in a blink. The Revere twins followed. And Hazel picked up her backpack and headed home, alone.

When Hazel walked in the house, her mom was sitting at the desk. She smiled when she saw her daughter. "Oh, honey, I just—"

And Hazel started to cry.

"What's wrong? Hazel, sweetie—"

Her mother's face looked stricken, as if seeing her daughter this way was the worst thing that could possibly happen, and Hazel could do nothing but tell her the truth.

"Jack isn't talking to me," she said.

Hazel's mom led her to the couch and sat down next to her. "What do you mean? Did you guys have a fight?"

"No!" Hazel exclaimed, wiping her eyes. "He just

stopped talking to me! He was *mean*."

"Oh, baby," her mom said, her voice cracking a little. "I'm so sorry."

"Something's wrong." Hazel said. "He wouldn't just do that. He's my best friend."

"Oh, Hazel." Her mother shook her head. "You know, this is so hard. It's one of the really hard things about growing up. Sometimes your friends change."

"What?"

"Well, sometimes when you get older you grow apart."

Hazel straightened and stared at her mother. "Overnight?"

She shrugged. "Maybe. You guys have been two peas in a pod for so long. Maybe Jack decided he needs to have some friends who are boys. It's natural for someone Jack's age."

"But . . . " Hazel said, "he *has* friends who are boys. He just likes me better."

Her mom gazed at her, lips pressed together, and Hazel could hear all the things she was not letting herself say. "Haze, dear," she said finally, "Jack's going through a lot, you know. It's got to be so hard for him."

"Yeah, but . . ." But that's why he needed her.

"You just wait and see what happens. If he's a true friend, he'll come back."

"He *is* a true friend!" Hazel mentally stomped her foot.

"Well, good." She stroked Hazel's shoulder. "And in the meantime you can make other friends. We're going to the Briggses' tomorrow, remember? You had fun with Adelaide, didn't you?"

Hazel felt the tears come again, and she put her head in her hands.

"Oh, sweetie," her mom said, hugging her. "This happens. I'm so sorry it happened to you."

And Hazel could see that she was sorry. She meant everything she said. But her mom didn't know. She didn't really know Jack. Jack was her best friend. He wasn't going to leave her because he was going through a lot. And he was not going to grow out of her overnight like she was an old puffy purple jacket.

It didn't make any sense at all.

Chapter Seven

THE WITCH

Once upon a time, there was a boy named Jack who lived in a small house on a placemat of a yard. He lived with his father, who held the whole house on his back, and his mother, whose eyes registered nothing when they looked at him. He was made of superheroes and castles and baseball, but sometimes he had trouble remembering that. One day the snow transformed the world around him into a different kind of place, and two days after that he got a piece of an enchanted mirror in his eye. The mirror went right to his heart. And then he changed.

But Jack didn't know anything was wrong. He felt suddenly wonderful, as if all the energies of the world were surging through him, as if he knew precisely what he was made of. He could barely get through the school day with his body crackling like it did. At the end of the day he bounded on the bus with his friends, brain and body abuzz with something like he had never felt before. And as he headed down the aisle, he felt the bus would not be able to go fast enough for him, no matter how hard it tried, and what he should have been doing was flying through the winter sky.

Instead, he tripped on a third grader's backpack.

"Smooth!" yelled Tyler as Jack stumbled.

"I meant to do that!" Jack yelled back. "And it was *awesome*!"

The third grader eyed Jack warily and inched his backpack out of the path. Jack grinned at him and winked. No one had anything to fear from him.

"What are we doing today?" Rico asked as the bus pulled out of the lot.

"We gotta go sledding!" Jack said.

Jack wasn't going to be inside, not today. All he wanted to do was be in the snow. At recess they'd made snow forts and had snowball fights and Jack was a master—his fort was bigger and thicker than everyone else's, and his snowballs seemed to have targeting computers on them. He got hit a lot, too, but he was a superhero and the snow just fueled his powers. He was the Snow Man, and he could be either hero or villain, Indomitable or Abominable. Both sides wanted him for his amazing powers—and neither wanted the other to have him. What would Jack choose?

"Yeah," said Tyler. "Bobby and Kai want to come. Kai's got a new sled, supposed to be super fast."

"Not as fast as me!" Rico said.

"Whatever," said Jack. "I'll beat any of you."

The boys agreed to meet at the sledding hill in an hour. Jack had to go home first because his father had made him promise he'd call right after school. Jack thought he was making a big deal about nothing. He barely remembered the accident. He had been at recess, he knew that much, and then something got in his eye. And then there was pain shooting from his eye to his chest. He remembered that part like you'd remember a story someone told to you once, like you might nod in sympathy but it wasn't like it happened to you.

He got to ride in an ambulance, though they didn't turn the sirens on. And then he was in the emergency room and there were doctors and at some point the pain just stopped, though he didn't remember if that was because they gave him something or not. And then he was home and the boys came over and it was like nothing had ever hurt him in his entire life or ever would.

It had taken him about fifteen minutes to do his homework that night. He only did the math and ignored everything else. Because the math he suddenly understood instinctively, like a truth. Fractions were like baseball statistics, three hits out of ten is .300 or 3/10. It was perfect.

Jack had trouble sitting still in school the next morning. He wanted to shout all the answers out, to explain to everyone what he now understood. But he didn't even have the words for it; he could just *see* it: 1/4 is .25 is 25 out of 100.

So Jack did problems in his head all day. A player who had 516 at-bats in a year would need 206 hits to bat .400. A catcher might have 100 fewer at bats, and would need 166 hits.

After the school bus dropped him off, he ran home and fixed himself a peanut-butter sandwich. And then another one. As he was eating the second, his mom wandered in the kitchen.

"You're home."

He put his sandwich down. "Yeah."

"How's your eye?"

"Fine."

"Good."

Silence. Then: "Are you going out?"

"Yeah, I'm going sledding."

"All right."

Jack looked sideways at his mother. Her pants were gross. Her hair was like a homeless person's. Her eyes were dead. Something flared up inside him, and he exhaled and shook his head. He saw something pass over her face.

"I gotta go," he muttered. And ran out the door.

He felt suddenly like he could not breathe, like the air no longer wanted anything to do with him. He went to the garage to get his sled. It looked beat up and flimsy. It was not good enough.

Jack dragged his sled around the corner and down the ten long blocks to the good park. The sky was touched with purple now, and the snow shone brightly against the dark background. The air smelled of cold. Everything was quiet, the only sound the crunching of Jack's boots and the soft drag of the sled. The noise he made assaulted his ears.

There was no one at the hill when he got there. The park was silent. Jack dragged his sled up to the top of the steep hill. He wasn't supposed to sled by himself, but no one was there to notice. And the trees in the wood behind the hill loomed so watchfully that it seemed he was not alone.

He placed his sled on the top of the hill, sat down on it, and pushed himself off. Down, down the hill he went, buffered by the cool breeze. He leaned back and went faster and faster. The sled reached the bottom of the hill and flew several more feet before skidding out. It was not fast enough. Jack carried the sled back up the hill.

This time he lay on his stomach, head first. He was absolutely not supposed to do it this way. But the trees wouldn't tell. And he pushed himself off and felt as if he were really flying now.

Still, it was not enough. He could not do it.

He dragged the sled back up and was surprised to realize that it had started snowing. He stood and watched the flakes descend around him. They touched down gently on the dark trees in the wood, and Jack found himself taking a step closer. And another.

The snowflakes landed on him like a blessing. Like they saw him and welcomed him. He could see them, too, every perfect symmetrical bit of them. They were icy assurances, proof that there was an order to things. You could crawl into the center of one and understand everything.

A gust of wind picked up in the woods, and the snow in front of it began to stir. It was like a small tornado had settled at the tree line, and snow began to whirl around faster and faster. Jack took a step back as the spinning column got bigger, and part of him wanted to run, but it was only a small part. For he understood he was seeing magic.

And indeed he was. For the snow was not snow anymore, but a woman—tall and lithe like a sketch, in a white fur cape and a white shimmering gown that looked so thin it would melt if you touched it. Hair like spun crystal framed

cream-colored skin. The woman stepped closer, revealing eyes as bright as the sun reflecting off snow. But they were cold things, and it was like looking for solace in frost.

Jack could not move as she walked toward him. It did not seem possible that she would be coming for him, but she was. Her eyes did not leave him, and in her cold gaze he found his breath again. The air welcomed him back.

"Are you real?" he asked, though it was a stupid thing to ask.

"I am," she said, her voice twinkling and melodic.

"How do you do that?" He motioned to the snow out of which she had come.

She was in front of him now, and Jack felt his chest expand and then freeze, an inhalation with no companion.

"Doesn't that take the fun out of it?" she said. She spoke slowly, and her voice was like a chain that pulled you gently closer. "To know how it is done?"

"No. I want to know. I want to understand things. I want to understand everything." He sounded so desperate to his own ears.

"I see. And what will you do when you understand everything? Will you share your knowledge to better the world?" Her eyes sparkled with mischief.

Her eyes sparkled, for him. Jack felt a smile on his face. "Maybe."

She leaned in, bringing coldness with her. "Or," she murmured, "will you keep it all for yourself?"

"You never know," Jack said. His heart filled. He could play this game, he understood it like he understood the numbers. Everything made sense. He was pleased with himself for keeping up with this woman made of ice.

"What if I told you that there was a place where there are extraordinary things, things with great power, things that could give you your heart's desire, things much bigger than this small, small world?"

Jack's heart sped up, and he knew he was not playing a game anymore. "Is there?" he demanded.

"There is. What you saw from me is only the beginning."

"You want to take me there?"

"I do. I could tell looking at you that you are destined to do great things."

"Really?"

"Oh, yes, my young friend. I can make you live on forever." She motioned to the wood and he saw there a gleaming white sleigh attached to winged white horses. And he understood how small this world really was.

He took a step forward, but something stopped him, something his heart was whispering.

"Wait," he said, looking up at the white witch. "Will I be gone for long?"

She smiled. "Oh, don't worry," she said. "They won't miss you at all."

"Okay!" He climbed into the sleigh and the woman appeared next to him. She took hold of the reins and looked down at him with a sly smile.

"Would you like some Turkish delight?" she asked.

"Huh?"

"Just a little joke," she said. "Let's go."

Chapter Eight

REASONS

The next morning, Hazel's mother bundled her off to Adelaide's house. She spoke in bright, shiny words, as if that might distract Hazel from all thoughts of Jack.

It did not work.

Hazel kept her eyes on Jack's house as they drove by. There was no sign of life. Maybe Jack was out already, maybe he'd gone sledding with the boys again. It was Saturday, and Saturday was a good day for sledding. At least it used to be.

On the way, her mom chattered on about Adelaide and the Briggses, as if there were nothing else Hazel could possibly think about. Apparently, when a hand came down and plucked your best friend from the chair next to you, all you had to do was wait for it to drop someone else in there, and then you could just go on. And they said Hazel was the one who thought too much about magic.

"So, what did you think of Adelaide's uncle?" her mother asked.

Hazel shrugged. "He's funny."

"He's a character, all right. He was just like that in college, too. He just never grew up. Some people don't have to. They're lucky." She cast a glance at Hazel. "Most people do, though."

"I like him," Hazel said. They were driving by the lake now, and a group of brightly plumaged girls were emerging from the warming house carrying skates and chirping to each other. Saturday was also a good day for skating, apparently.

"Well, good. You think you can have fun today?"

"Sure," Hazel said.

"Try for me, okay?"

"Okay." Soon they arrived at the Briggses'. Today the house shone so brightly it hurt Hazel's eyes, and she wondered if it would even allow her in. If Jack thought she was a baby, what was Adelaide going to think?

Adelaide opened the door, smiling. Hazel hesitated. She wanted to keep this moment when Adelaide thought she was someone she would like to welcome in.

But there was nothing to do but enter the house, and Hazel found herself in the vast living room with Adelaide and her little brother, Jeremy, who was sitting at a desk poking around at a computer with a screen bigger than Hazel's TV.

"Mom wants us to watch him," Adelaide explained. "Sometimes he breaks things."

Hazel did not know how to respond to that. She didn't know anything about little brothers, except from books. She would have liked a brother or a little sister, but her parents had already traveled to another planet to get her. It's hard to do that twice.

"I break things, too," she said finally. And then flushed. This was the part where you were supposed to say something fascinating, if you were the sort of person that had fascinating things to say. This was not the part where you say *I break things, too*. "Um," she said, shifting. "I liked the story you were working on. With your uncle."

There. That was something. People liked compliments.

"Yeah!" Adelaide's eyes sparkled underneath her glasses. "That was cool. I want to be a writer, too. And a ballet dancer. I'm going to write stories and make ballets about them."

"Really?" Hazel didn't know that that was something you could do.

"Wanna do one now?"

"A . . . ballet?"

"Yeah! We could make one about the Snow Queen!"

"Um." Hazel bit her lip. "I . . . don't know how to dance."

"I'll teach you! Come on!"

In a few minutes Hazel was wearing one of Adelaide's leotards and ballet slippers, and was holding onto the back of a chair while Adelaide moved her feet around in various positions—first, second, third, fourth, fifth. Hazel's feet responded slowly, warily, unused to the attention. Then Adelaide stood in front of Hazel, positioned her own feet, stuck her arm in the air in an arc like a swan's neck, and bent her legs so she slowly dropped toward the ground.

"Wow," said Hazel.

"It's a plié. You do it on all the positions. It's very good for dramatic moments. Do you want to learn leaps?"

She did. They pushed all the furniture out of the way, and soon the girls were leaping around the room. Hazel's feet in the soft pink ballet slippers felt borrowed, like she would have to give them back. But she leapt anyway, and while the lamps shook and the decorative furniture quavered, she did not break a thing.

Hazel had feathers, she had wings, she had beautiful borrowed feet. If she could steal beauty from swans, even for a moment, maybe there was some kind of hope.

And then there was a mournful noise, and a clunking sound, and Adelaide's little brother's head was buried in his arms on the desk. He lifted it up, sighed dramatically, then clunked it down again.

Adelaide stopped. "Jer, what is it?"

He lifted his head enough to say, "Adie, you were gonna help me with my homework!"

The girls came to earth. "All right," Adelaide said. "What's your homework?"

"I'm supposed to write a bi-o-graph-y. It has to be a scientist, I can't make anything up, and I can't do Spider-man." He threw up his hands in despair.

"A scientist?" Adelaide screwed her face up in thought. "Um . . . Albert Einstein?"

"Everyone's going to do him! I want to be *special*!"

"Um . . . "Adelaide turned to Hazel. "Can you think of anyone?"

Hazel's heart stirred. Here was her chance. She might not be fascinating, her feet might be wary and slow, but maybe she could at least be useful. That would be something.

And then something whispered in one distant corner of her brain, and a picture of Mrs. Jacobs at the overhead flashed behind her eyes. "I know!" she said, jumping from first to third position. "There's a guy. Snowflake Something.

He was a scientist who took pictures of—"

"No!" came a voice from the kitchen. "No, no, no!"

Adelaide and Hazel exchanged a glance. "Uncle Martin," Adelaide mouthed.

Her uncle burst into the room, emphatically waving a pen. "Snowflake Bentley was *not* a scientist. Who said that?"

"I did," Hazel said in a small voice.

He smiled brightly. "Oh, hi, Hazel, it's nice to see you."

"Uncle Martin," Adelaide said, "I'm supposed to tell you when you're being weird."

"But this is a bridge too far! She's spreading lies!" He pointed dramatically at Hazel, and then shot her a wink.

"Wait," Hazel protested, "my teacher said—"

"Your teacher is wrong. Snowflake Bentley was not a scientist. He was a *farmer*. He looked at snowflakes under a microscope and realized that they were each unique. 'Miracles of beauty,' he called them. And he thought it was a tragedy that these tiny miracles would disappear. So he figured out how to take pictures of them. He wanted them to live forever." Martin turned dramatically to Jeremy. "Snowflake Bentley. Look him up on your precious Internet. Now!"

The boy turned and started to type, his finger hunting out each letter. Martin went over to him and leaned over his shoulder. "Here! 'When a snowflake melted,' he said, 'that design was forever lost. Just that much beauty was gone.' He was no scientist. He was a poet! How's that for your biography, Jeremy?"

The boy slumped in his chair. "I'd rather have Spider-man."

Martin flung his hands in the air. "Fine. I'll go where I'm appreciated. Nice to see you, Hazel." He turned toward the kitchen.

"Wait!" Hazel said. Uncle Martin turned, and Adelaide looked at Hazel in surprise. Hazel had surprised herself, too.

"Can I ask you something?" The words stuck in her throat.

Uncle Martin was the sort of person who understood things. He knew about the things that lived just beyond the boundary of what you could see. Hazel's wings twitched.

"Of course you may."

"Um . . ." Hazel shot a glance at Adelaide, who was giving her a curious look. She took a deep breath. ". . . Can you think of any reasons someone would . . . change over-night?"

He tilted his head. "Change how?"

"I mean," she said, as her heart jumped up in her throat and settled there, "they just don't act like themselves anymore? That they were nice and then suddenly they aren't anymore?"

Martin nodded slowly. "So, you mean a complete personality change."

"Yes."

"And might I guess that you are looking for reasons that aren't . . . natural?"

She exhaled. She wouldn't have said it out loud. "That's right."

"Well"—he rubbed his hands together—"let's see. There are a few options here. Possession is one. Maybe not by a demon, but by something a little more harmless, like a goblin or imp."

"Or a troll!" Jeremy exclaimed.

"Trolls don't possess people," Adelaide said, rolling her eyes at her brother.

"Or an evil corporate disembodied brain thing," Martin continued. "Or there could be some sort of enchantment. By a witch or wizard. Or by a magical item, something that was given to them, or something they acquired, maybe by accident. Or something that's infected them that causes them to see the world in a skewed way."

"A poison apple," said Adelaide.

"A magic potion," said Hazel.

"Yes. Precisely. Or someone could have some kind of

magical hold on this person, like spiritual blackmail. Or maybe they're in the process of transforming into something else."

"A turtle!" said Jeremy.

"He means a werewolf," said Adelaide.

"Either way. Does that help?" Martin asked.

Hazel nodded, heart pounding. She took a deep breath, looking from Jeremy to Adelaide to Uncle Martin. "Do you . . ." she said to the man, her voice quiet, "do you believe that these things can happen?"

Martin nodded thoughtfully. "I believe that the world isn't always what we can see," he said. "I believe there are secrets in the woods. And I believe that goodness wins out." He gave Hazel a serious look. "So, if someone's changed overnight—by witch curse or poison apple or were-turtle—you have to show them what's good. You show them love. That works a surprising amount of the time. And if that doesn't save them, they're not worth saving."

Hazel nodded slowly. Out of the corner of her eye she saw Adelaide nod, too, as if this information might be useful to her some day.

"Did you have fun?" Hazel's mother asked in the car on the way home.

"Yes," Hazel said.

"Good. Me, too."

"Mom?"

"Yeah?"

"Um"—under her seat she moved her left foot forward so the heel touched on the arch of the right—"can I take ballet lessons?"

Her mom glanced at her. "Ballet?" she repeated.

"Adelaide takes ballet."

"Oh." Her mother's eyes fell closed for a moment. "Hazel, baby," she began, and Hazel never would have asked if she'd known how sad her mom would look. "I'd *love* to give you ballet lessons. But . . . they cost money, and . . ." She shook her head. "Maybe someday? When things are a little better?"

Hazel gulped and nodded, looking carefully at a spot on the dashboard.

"I suppose . . ." Her mom hesitated. "I suppose I could ask your father."

Hazel looked up. "Really?"

"I can *ask*," she repeated.

Hazel nodded, moving her feet into first position. In her mind she executed a grand plié.

"Mom?"

"Yes?"

"Do you think I should do something? About Jack, I mean?" Hazel didn't know what that something might be—a letter, a present, convincing Joe Mauer to show up on his doorstep? Something. Something that was good.

Her mother's eyes flicked over her. She seemed to start to say something, and then stopped. "Oh, honey," she said finally. "Sometimes there's just nothing you can do."

Hazel's eyes darted to the window. Her heart plummeted, and her feathers fell away.

She could be such a baby sometimes.

Chapter Nine

SLEIGH RIDE

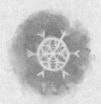

Jack and the white witch took off in the sleigh, and in the blink of an eye they were in the woods behind the sledding hill. Jack had been in these woods many times, but they had never been like this. These woods seemed as if they must have been there since the beginning of time. Trees stretched up into the darkening sky like yearning giants, their thick branches contorted and mean from reaching out for something they could never grasp. Snow lay heavily on the branches like shrouds. The bloated moon lurked above the tangled mass of branches.

The wind sang softly to him, like a whispered lullaby. He thought he heard it carrying his name from somewhere in the far distance, as if an echo from a memory. And then it was gone.

The witch held the reins, steering the sled surely through the trees as if they were no obstacle at all, as if they were not even there. And Jack saw that the creatures pulling the sleigh were not winged horses at all, but a pack of horse-size white wolves with fur that glimmered in the moonlight. They bolted ahead, sleek and sure, and their energy made the sleigh feel alive. Jack could hear the steady panting of the wolves as their breath echoed in their chests. It was the only sound that accompanied the distant lullaby of the wind, and it made it seem as if the whole forest was breathing.

The witch looked ahead. He wanted to say something to her, to tell her something so she would know she had made a good choice in him.

"I can do numbers in my head," he said.

"Can you, now?"

"Even fractions."

"My," she said.

"I know the stats for all the batting title winners. I know the populations of Minneapolis and St. Paul. I can convert centimeters into inches. I can do word problems—ask me anything."

His words sounded foolish to his own ears. He was not

impressive. He was small like the world.

"I feel like I'm forgetting something," he said. "Do you think my mom is worried?"

The witch looked down at him and smiled, and he knew he would do anything to earn that smile. "No. You don't have to worry about her anymore."

"And my friends?"

"They will be fine without you," she said.

"I think I'm cold."

"My poor boy," she said. "Come here." In a swift motion she tucked him into her furs, and it was like being wrapped in snow. He could not tell if he was warmer or if he just didn't notice the cold as much, but it did not matter. She was taking care of him, even though he was nothing. And she was happy, too—she laughed and kissed his forehead like his mother used to do when she tucked him in at night. It had been a long time since she had done that.

When her lips touched his skin, he sucked in an involuntary, desperate breath and a weight slammed into his chest. His body seized up as a great shudder overtook him, and somewhere in his young mind he knew it was like death.

And then in a blink everything at his center was at peace, and he could not remember if any of it had happened at all. It would have been a strange thing to happen.

He smiled at the witch, who ran a cool hand across his cheek and gave him one more kiss.

"Now you may have no more kisses," the witch said, "or I'll kiss you to death!"

And they drove on. He felt the cold less and less, and everything else, too. He did not know if they were still in the forest or flying through the sky. They were both, somehow. He remembered, distantly, the life he had before this. It seemed a funny sort of thing, like a joke with a forgotten punch line.

By the time they came to her palace, he felt nothing at all.

Chapter Ten

SLUSH

Hazel spent the rest of the weekend glancing out the window, but she never saw any signs of life at Jack's house. His mother always kept the shades drawn now, so Hazel could see nothing inside. She never heard his garage door open or the car go out. The house seemed as dark and closed up as Jack was.

When Hazel woke up on Monday morning, dread slammed into her like a oncoming truck. She did not want to go to school. She considered pretending to be sick, but her mom would never buy it. Hazel could see the whole conversation play out in her head—*I know it's hard, honey, but sometimes we have to do hard things in life*. Even if she were actually sick, her mother wouldn't believe her. She could be seriously ill, she could be doubled over with an exploded appendix, and her mother would say that sometimes we have to do hard things in life and that she had to face Jack eventually anyway, so she might as well do it with an exploded appendix.

At least Jack wasn't in her class. What seemed a tragedy in the beginning of the year was now a blessing. She would just go through the rest of the year not talking to anyone. She could read during recess, that would be okay. She had a lot of books to read. It would just be like she was a leper, and leprosy really wasn't so bad once you made it part of your routine.

She couldn't get out of school, but there was one thing she absolutely could not face this morning. So as soon as her mother entered the kitchen that morning, Hazel asked:

"Mom? Will you drive me to school today?"

"Why? . . . Oh." Her face fell. "Honey, I just can't. I'm so sorry, I have a call." She squeezed Hazel's shoulder. "I know it's going to be hard, but you have to face Jack sometime. It might as well be today. And . . . you can sit with someone else on the bus! You can show him you don't need him."

Hazel did not understand. Her mom kept going on and on about how this kind of thing happens all the time. But apparently it had never happened to her.

"Okay. Thanks, Mom."

So Hazel lingered by the front door as long as she possibly could, then, after some nudging from her mother, trudged out to the bus stop. She kept her eyes straight ahead as she passed Jack's house. A wraith struck her with its death-touched blade and the poison caused her heart to go cold. She could feel nothing, and above all she absolutely could not cry. She could not cry.

It had gotten warmer overnight. The street was shiny and cars kicked up chunks of gray muck. The snow was half-slush, and what had been pristine and white was now slimy and depressing.

She approached the bus stop with her eyes focused on the ground ahead of her, because footprints were very interesting and should be studied closely. But Jack wasn't there. The Revere twins stood alone together, poking each other as usual. Hazel moved to the edge of the sidewalk and concentrated on the odd effects of her wraith-poisoned heart.

Hazel waited for the crunch-slosh of Jack's approach, marveling at the coldness at her center. And the bright yellow bus came around the corner, and Jack still had not come. She could not help looking down the street to see if his blue-clad form was running toward them, but there was no one there.

"Where's Tweedledum?" asked the bus driver as she walked on.

"I don't know," she replied.

Hazel went back and sat in her seat in the middle of the bus and got out her book.

Maybe he didn't want to see her, either.

Having a cloud of venomous coldness where her heart used to be changed everything for Hazel. When she walked into Mrs. Jacobs's class she surveyed her fellow students with impassive interest. Her eyes fell on Tyler and Bobby, and she did not blush and turn away or menace them with school supplies. She just eyed them coolly, as if they were nothing to her, as if their nothingness surprised and slightly repelled her.

Bobby was smirking at her, she noted, and she deduced that it was a smirk of victory. And Tyler—Tyler had another expression on his face altogether. He was staring at her intently, his brown eyes wide, his eyebrows locked, his lips smooshed together. He looked like he was trying to decide something, and the process was a bit painful.

Hazel cocked her head at him quizzically. He sighed, shook his head slightly, and turned back to Bobby.

She had no trouble paying attention to Mrs. Jacobs that morning. Her eyes never wandered out the window to the slushy world beyond. Everything the teacher said seemed to make sense and be very relevant to the world around her—sentences needed to be diagrammed and fractions must be multiplied and the mysteries of the earth could be explained by an endless cycle of evaporation, condensation, and precipitation. School was very easy, it turned out, if you just disconnected your heart.

The clock ticked on dispassionately. When it was time for recess Hazel got up slowly and carefully put on her outdoor things and filed out in an orderly fashion with the rest of her class. She took up position in a discrete corner of the playground, which she calculated was the best place to observe the door without being seen.

The big slide looked lonely, she noted.

She watched Mr. Williams's class file out of the school, looking for Jack's form. She would see where he went, and then go the opposite direction. It was a good plan, the sort of plan you can make when you are thinking with your head and not your dissolved heart. That is the thing with curses—they seem like a bad thing at first, but then sometimes you realize you can't live without them.

And then the whole class was out, and Jack wasn't there. *How curious,* Hazel thought. *How odd.* The facts, as Hazel had observed them, were that Jack was not on the bus, was not at his desk, and was not at recess. The logical conclusion was that Jack was not in school today.

Hazel's eyes traveled across the playground and landed

on the crew of boys. They were already running around, pushing each other into the slush. All except one—Tyler was staring at the quiet doorway, just as she had been.

His head turned slowly and his eyes met hers. He looked at her for three blinks, and then turned away.

Curious.

At lunch, Hazel sat in a corner, stirring her macaroni and cheese with her fork and studying the people around her. They had a tendency to congregate in pairs and groups. For instance, at the next table over from her sat Molly and Susan, whispering to each other and giggling. They were two, like Hazel and Jack used to be. At the other end of the table was a trio of fourth-grade girls—one in orange, one in green, one in yellow, like the vegetable medley on their trays. They were three, and Hazel wondered what would happen if a big hand came and plucked one of them away. Would the other two be able to go on as before, nodding every once in a while to the ghost of the third, or would the sudden change in gravity cause the other two to just float away?

"Hazel?"

Hazel turned around. Mikaela was standing behind her, holding her tray. Her Jell-O cubes quivered uncertainly.

"Yes?" Hazel responded, in the way that you do.

"Um"—Mikaela looked around—"Jack's not here today?"

Ah. Mikaela had not taken the time to observe the facts. This is the sort of thing that leads to stupid questions. "No, he's not."

She frowned. "I didn't think so. Is he okay?"

Hazel frowned back. "I really don't know," she said. "I don't have the information."

"Oh," said Mikaela. "Because it seemed like he really got hurt on Friday."

"It did," agreed Hazel.

"Well, um, I hope he's okay."

Hazel blinked. It occurred to her that Mikaela was being nice to her. She did not know how to react, for when your heart has been poisoned and someone picks a dandelion for you—because it is bright and yellow and you seem like you could use something like that—all you can do is contemplate the funny ways of weeds.

Mikaela glanced at the empty seat next to Hazel, then at Hazel. The Jell-O jiggled. "Can I sit with you?"

"Oh. Sure."

Mikaela put her tray down and settled in next to her. She did not stick green beans in her nose as Jack would have done, but Hazel did not really expect her to.

"I guess they're friends again," she said, pointing to Molly and Susan.

"That's what the facts seem to indicate," Hazel said.

Mikaela blinked at her, and then looked back at the other table. "It's hard to keep track sometimes."

Hazel nodded, as if she knew what the girl meant.

Mikaela asked a few more questions about Jack and Hazel responded, as people do. There was a boyish yelping from a few tables away, and Mikaela's eyes darted over there and then back. Hazel's eyes followed. Mikaela saw and leaned into Hazel.

"You know Bobby's a jerk, right?"

She looked like she wanted an answer, and so Hazel nodded. She did know. The facts indicated that, too.

"You shouldn't listen to him. I mean, what he said yesterday. You know."

Hazel knew.

"It's funny. We used to play all the time together, like in kindergarten and stuff."

"Oh," said Hazel. "What happened?"

Mikaela tilted her head for a moment and then shrugged. "I'm not sure."

Just then Susan's voice called Mikaela's name from the next table. Hazel watched as Mikaela looked up.

Susan beckoned. "Come eat with us!"

Mikaela blinked at her and looked at Hazel.

"It's okay," said Hazel. "I was just about finished."

"Okay. 'Bye, Hazel."

"Good-bye."

Mikaela got up and moved over to join Susan and Molly. The two became three, and Hazel carefully studied the shift in gravity.

When she got back to her classroom, Mrs. Jacobs stopped her. "The counselor's office sent up a note," she said. "You have an appointment tomorrow morning, during recess."

"Thank you very much," said Hazel.

Mrs. Jacobs regarded her. "You're very welcome, Hazel."

They had art class that afternoon. The walls of the room were lined with galleries from each grade, and on the fifth-grade wall two of Jack's pieces were at the very top. At one time, this had made Hazel very proud.

Their art teacher was named Ms. Blum, though in her head Hazel had always called her Mrs. Whatsit, because she wore weird baggy clothes and seemed like the sort of person who might tesser in some dark and stormy night. It seemed now an odd thing to think.

Ms. Blum was introducing their new project, speaking, as she always did, with grand hand gestures that Hazel used to find dramatic but now made her fear for the jars of paint.

"I've noticed," said Ms. Blum, her hands in the air, "that we've all been spending time making art about things we know. But you don't have to just make a picture of something you know, something real. So for our next project I want you to show me a place that isn't real, something you make up."

Hazel frowned along with the rest of the class.

One of the girls raised her hand. "Like . . . pretend?"

"Yes," said Ms. Blum. "This is what artists do all the time. They, like, pretend. They don't have to just show the world as it is. You can use art to express something. . . . Think of an emotion or an idea and make a place that evokes that idea."

Hazel stared at the paint-splotted table in front of her. There was a time when she would have loved this assignment, when she had a thousand made-up places at her fingertips just waiting for someone to ask to see them. But now she could think of nothing. There were so many real places in the world, and they had so much weight to them. There were front hallways and bus stops and the space on the other side of classroom doors. There were lonely big slides and microscopically out of line desks and lunch tables that survived gravity shifts. How could anyone ever make something up?

She moved to the supply table with the rest of the class,

able to see nothing but the world as it was.

She took a piece of plain white paper and stared at it. It was an empty, inhospitable thing. Hazel exhaled. And then she remembered Jack's sketch.

Hazel drew a tiny fort in the middle of the page—an austere palace framed by four tall turrets. In Hazel's hands they looked a little like deformed lollipops. Then she drew a long line coming out from either side of the palace, stretching out across the landscape of the paper.

Hazel felt the presence of the teacher behind her.

"That's your sketch?" Ms. Blum asked.

Hazel nodded. The thing with not being able to draw very well is you didn't have to spend any time at it.

"What colors are you going to use?" Ms. Blum motioned to the paint wall.

"Just white," said Hazel.

The teacher stared at the drawing, and then gave Hazel a searching look.

"This is different for you," she said.

"It's a fort," Hazel explained. "No one can ever find you there."

"That's very interesting, Hazel," the teacher finally said.

"Thank you, Ms. Blum," said Hazel.

❄

A second-grade girl sat next to Hazel on the bus and started showing her her sticker collection. The boys were already in the back, but there was no Jack there, either. Hazel wondered what had happened to him. Maybe Jack was pretending to be sick. But that wasn't logical—it wasn't like Jack was upset. He was completely happy to be a total jerk.

Maybe his father had kept him home for the day, just to be safe. His father worried a lot more, now.

It was possible that he was actually sick. Maybe he got hurt worse than anyone knew. And no one was telling her. She had no information at all. He could be in the hospital hooked up to tubes and beeping things with people in scrubs standing over him whispering dramatically and scribbling on clipboards, and she would have no idea, no one would tell her. Maybe she should go visit him, maybe he needed her, maybe when he saw her the beeping would get stronger and Jack would sit up in bed and the doctors would gasp and scribble about the miracle before their eyes.

The poison lifted. Her heart breathed free. And—

"Are you okay?" the second grader asked, closing her sticker album.

Hazel swallowed and turned to stare out the window at the slushy gray real world.

❄

On the way from the bus stop, Hazel walked by Jack's house slowly. She tried to sneak glances at the front windows while at the same time making a show of looking straight ahead. It was not easy.

And then, from behind her, the sound of a car. Hazel turned. The red station wagon was pulling up in the driveway. Hazel felt a wave rise up inside of her and crash. Jack's parents got out of the car and began to walk toward the house. No Jack.

Hazel took a deep breath and called out, "Mr. and Mrs. Campbell?"

They turned around. Mr. Campbell had his hand lightly on his wife's back. Hazel didn't even know she ever left the house.

"Um, is Jack okay? He wasn't in school. And—"

And what? And he was mean.

And, that.

Jack's mother gave her a hazy smile. Something about it made Hazel's stomach rotate a few degrees. She seemed more human, but still somehow wrong, like they'd gotten the souls mixed up and put the wrong one back inside her.

"Oh, yes," Mr. Campbell said. "He's just fine."

"Oh."

What did Hazel expect? *He went temporarily insane and we took him to a doctor and he got a pill and now he's better and wants to see you?*

"He's just gone away for a while," Mrs. Campbell added.

Hazel blinked. "What?"

"He's gone to live with his dear elderly aunt Bernice," she said, voice gaining strength. "She needs help, you see. He's doing just fine, and we needn't worry."

She smiled at Hazel again, and both parents turned and disappeared into the house.

Chapter Eleven

MAGICAL THINKING

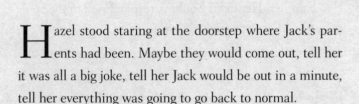

Hazel stood staring at the doorstep where Jack's parents had been. Maybe they would come out, tell her it was all a big joke, tell her Jack would be out in a minute, tell her everything was going to go back to normal.

But they didn't.

Hazel replayed the words Mrs. Campbell had spoken, trying to find the sense in them. But there wasn't any.

Her mother agreed. "I didn't even know he *had* an elderly aunt," she said, after Hazel told her what had happened.

"Me neither," said Hazel.

"Maybe she means *great*-aunt. But why would they send Jack? I mean, what about *school*?"

"I don't know," said Hazel.

"And it's not like he's particularly qualified for elder care. I mean, he's *eleven*. What do they expect him to do, teach her to play Zombie Assault?"

"I don't know," said Hazel, shifting a little. She was beginning to feel like it was her fault.

"*Weird.*" Her mom shook her head. "They have to be making it up. But why wouldn't they make up something *believable*? I mean, his elderly aunt is named *Bernice*." She shook her head again. "And Mrs. Campbell told you this? How did she seem?"

"Um . . . " Her mom wouldn't respond well to the soul-switching theory. "Kind of . . . weird."

Hazel's mother sighed. "I suppose it's none of our business. Maybe it was better to have him away right now. It has to be so hard on him. But at least this will make it easier for you, right? Not to have to see him all the time?"

Hazel looked at her feet.

"Come on, hon. I'll make some pasta." She let out a small laugh. "I know, I know. For a change."

"Mom?" Hazel pointed her toe. "What if he doesn't come back?"

Her mother put her hand on Hazel's shoulder and looked into her eyes. "Then you'll be okay. You will. Now, come with me." She straightened and motioned to the kitchen. "I'll teach you how to boil noodles."

Hazel smiled a little. "And microwave some sauce?"

"Don't get carried away," said her mom. "I can't give you all my cooking secrets in one day."

Hazel looked down at her feet, poised in perfect third position, and then undid them and followed her mom into the kitchen.

When Hazel woke up on Tuesday morning, the truth of things finally hit her. Jack was gone. Just gone. He didn't call her, or come over, or leave a note, or anything. He didn't say good-bye, because he didn't care to. He didn't try to explain the things he said, or the way he acted. He was perfectly happy to leave her feeling like this. And there was no witch, no wraith blade, no evil corporate brain-thingy that had caused the change in him. He had just changed. He just didn't like her anymore.

And that meant, even if Jack came back from his elderly aunt—or wherever he was—he was still gone.

She dragged herself down to the kitchen for breakfast to find her mother sitting at the small breakfast table waiting for her, with a face that made Hazel think she should turn right around and crawl back into bed until summer.

"Sit down, hon. I need to talk to you."

Hazel slid into the hard chair.

"I talked to your father," her mom continued, and Hazel's eyes snapped to the long gouge she'd made in the table when she was seven and wanted to play Excalibur. "I'm so sorry. About the ballet lessons. Your dad says he can't do it right now. With the wedding, you know . . ."

Hazel moved her head in an approximation of a nod.

Her mother exhaled, and moved to put her hand on Hazel's. Hazel did not let herself blink. "About your dad . . . you know . . ." Her voice was fraying from the strain of picking words so carefully. "I know he's not being that . . . communicative now, but that's his way. If he's not calling you, it's not because he doesn't want to . . . but because he feels . . . bad. I wish it were different. Believe me. But it doesn't mean he doesn't love you to the stars, do you understand?"

Hazel near-nodded again. The scar on the table blurred.

"We'll get you lessons someday, hon. I promise."

"I better go," Hazel said, standing up from the chair. "I'll be late."

At the bus stop, Hazel took her spot at the edge of the sidewalk, a few feet away from the twins. When the bus came, she boarded it with her eyes down. This is how she was going to get through the seven-hour leper-o-rama of school—with her eyes always on the ground.

Of course, she'd just bump into people.

Immediately when she walked down the aisle of the

bus she felt eyes boring into her. She looked up and saw Tyler staring at her.

Hazel wished she had something in her hands to throw. She looked away and sat down.

She opened up the new library book she'd brought for the bus ride and willed her thoughts to disappear in the pages. The girl in it was reading *A Wrinkle in Time.* She was best friends with a boy who lived in the apartment below. And then one day the boy stopped talking to her. Hazel closed the book.

When the bus arrived at school, Hazel gathered her things slowly, waiting for everyone else to get off. But when she got off she found Tyler waiting for her.

"What?" she snapped.

"Um, Jack's not here today either?"

"Doesn't look like it, no."

"Do you know where he is?"

So that's what this is about. He couldn't call over there himself? Couldn't boys do anything by themselves?

"He went to stay with his elderly aunt Bernice," Hazel responded primly. "She's sickly and she needs his help." Hazel smiled in the way people who have superior information do, and walked away.

When she passed Mr. Williams's classroom, she did not stop to look in.

As she walked into her class, she wondered if people noticed the change in her, if you could extract such a big part of yourself but still look the same on the outside, or if people would notice that she was part girl, part hollowed-out space.

Hazel sat down, ignoring the presence of the boys behind her. Mikaela smiled a greeting at her, and the girl part of Hazel smiled a little back, because that's what you do. And then the hollowed-out part took over, and Hazel settled in for a Jack-less day.

As Mrs. Jacobs yammered on that morning, Hazel found her eyes drawn to the busy street out the window. This is what there was in the world, busy streets thick with the smell of car exhaust and fast-food hamburgers. Maybe everyone was right, maybe she did let her imagination run away with her, and maybe she could be a baby sometimes.

Then it was time for recess, and Hazel girded herself. She got up and was heading outside with everyone else when Mrs. Jacobs stopped her.

"Hazel?"

She looked.

"Don't forget you have your appointment today."

Mrs. Jacobs put a slight emphasis on the word *appointment*, so Hazel would understand that this was not an appointment with a hair stylist or a dentist or a vet, but the sort of appointment that causes you to articulate the word a little more carefully.

"Crazy Hazy," someone muttered.

So, while her classmates filed outside, Hazel slung her backpack over her shoulder and trudged down the hall to the counselor's office.

To get to Mr. Lewis's office, you had to walk across the third floor and up the stairs into a corridor Hazel had never been in. It seemed like the sort of place that should be guarded by a three-headed dog. It didn't seem like part of school anymore—the corridor was thickly carpeted, and the walls were painted a chipper light blue and tastefully decorated with black-and-white photos of flowers. There was a small waiting area—just two chairs and a table with a big flower arrangement. Hazel leaned in to smell the flowers. They were fake. She put her hand out and rubbed a white petal between her hands. It was rough and plastic-y. What was the point?

"Hazel Anderson?"

Hazel pulled her hand back. A small man with round glasses, big cheeks, and a ring of thin brown-gray hair was looking at her as if she were doing something very peculiar. He looked like a chipmunk.

If Jack were here, Hazel would tell him about the

chipmunk counselor, and he would draw a cartoon of a chipmunk with big glasses behind a desk and the chipmunk would say, "I'm so sorry, Hazel, but you're nuts."

Mr. Lewis welcomed her into his office and sat down behind a big desk. He motioned Hazel into one of the yellow armchairs in front of the desk. She sat down, clutching her backpack to herself.

The window on the other side of his desk looked out on the playground. Hazel had to will herself to look at the chipmunk man and not the thick, winter-white sky.

Mr. Lewis had a file on his desk, and Hazel knew that that file represented her, that when she became a hollowed-out thing this file would seem to be the sum total of her existence on the planet. And there would be no one around to tell anyone any different.

"So, do you know why you're here?" Mr. Lewis asked, eyes blinking rapidly behind his glasses.

She didn't, particularly, but she knew that some questions were best answered untruthfully.

"I threw a pencil case," she said.

"At one of your classmates."

"Yes."

"Do you often find yourself feeling angry?"

Hazel crossed her arms. She felt like she was being poked. "Everyone does," she said quietly.

"Everyone gets angry, Hazel. Not everyone throws things at people."

It was the whole point, wasn't it? Hazel was not like everyone else. She was surprised that that wasn't in the file.

"Do you want to tell me what happened?"

Hazel shifted. "I was upset. My friend had gotten hurt."

"You've been here a few months now. Do you feel like you're fitting in here, Hazel?"

Hazel squirmed. She did not know how she was supposed to survive things like this anymore.

Mr. Lewis flipped through her file and kept asking her questions, and she knew what the notes in the file said just as surely as if she was reading them herself. This is what would be left of Hazel Anderson once her whole body hollowed out, the empty shell of her cracked, and the pieces flew to the winds: *Hazel has anger issues. She has trouble following rules. She does not pay attention. She has an overactive imagination. She has trouble making friends. She does not fit, not anywhere.*

She felt like a bird that someone was preparing to stuff and put on the mantel. He would have small dinner parties and show off his new wonder, and the guests would marvel that her dull eyes once contained life, and he would carefully describe to them the process of taking out her insides, piece by piece, and the very odd quality her heart had when you held it up to the light.

And then the questions were done, and Mr. Lewis closed the file and leaned into her, rodent-y eyes squinting. "Hazel. You're a smart girl. May I speak frankly?"

He looked at her like he genuinely expected an answer. "Okay."

"A lot has happened to you this year. The change in schools. The upheaval in your family. But you're eleven now. I think you can take control."

"Okay."

"And maybe there are things you need help with. We want to look at the attention issues, certainly. And the mood issues. We're going to figure out what you need. And you can take ownership. For instance, we could draw up a plan, and if you needed to put yourself in time-out, you could."

"Time-out?"

"Yes. You know. If you find yourself feeling angry in class. You could just leave the classroom. A time-out."

"Oh." Everyone else wanted Hazel to be more grown up, now the counselor was giving her a time out.

"So here's what's going to happen now. I'm going to make some referrals. There are a couple of different ave- nues I want to pursue. We should have a meeting with your mother. We're all going to be partners here."

He said this like it was a good thing, like Hazel would

really want to be partners with this chipmunk man. He made some notes and added them to her file, making it bigger while she got smaller.

He dismissed her, and Hazel poured concrete into the hollow parts. Now she would be part girl, part hardening gray sludge. And no one would notice the difference.

After the bus let her off, Hazel found herself heading in the opposite direction from her house—down a couple of neighborhood blocks, around the funny lime-green house with the tiny white fence, down the hill to the railroad tracks. She kicked up slush as she walked, and her jeans were wet and spattered by the time she arrived at the field where the shrieking shack was.

The once-white field was now made of wet, slurpy snow. Their footprints had disappeared, but there were new ones in their place—three sets of heavy-booted adult-size prints. Hazel chewed on her lip and took a few steps closer to the shack, which was now dark and wet with melting snow. She didn't know what she was doing there, but she didn't have anywhere else to go, and sometimes you need to hole up in the decaying floor of a ruined old shack and pour concrete into your hollow places.

But as Hazel walked toward the house she realized the air was vibrating with noise. She was not alone. There were people in her house, and they were laughing and yelling and their voices were rough and loud and had the sharp edges of crushed-up beer cans.

Hazel stopped and took a step back from the house. She stood there for a moment, looking at the lonely, broken-down thing. It was a palace once.

And then she turned around and began to trudge home.

Chapter Twelve

Passages

When Hazel got home that afternoon, she found the house empty. This was the first year her mother had let her stay by herself, and she'd used to like being in the house on her own. But she had had enough of empty spaces today. And, anyway, her mom was the last one left.

The house felt strange. Altered. Like someone had come in during the day and shrunk all the furniture just a tiny bit. Or she'd gone through a closet door and come out in the living room of her button-eyed Other Mother.

Of course things like that did not actually happen. Not in the real world.

Hazel was heading to her room when the phone rang. Her mom, probably, asking Hazel to preheat the oven for some frozen slab of something. She went over to the desk and picked up the phone.

There was a moment of silence on the other end. The phone crackled. And then a voice: "Oh, Hazel . . . hi."

Hazel's fingers tightened around the phone. "Hi, Dad."

"How are you?"

"Fine."

"Good. How's school?"

"Good."

"Good. Good. I was thinking I should come visit you."

"Really?"

"Yes. I miss my princess."

"When are you coming?"

"You know how it is right now. After the wedding, though. And you're going to come up for that, right?"

"I guess so."

"Great. I can't wait to see you, princess. Is your mom there?"

"No. She's not home yet."

"Okay. Tell her I called."

"Okay."

And Hazel hung up and shuffled off to her room.

The next two days passed like this for Hazel—Jack-lessness and empty spaces and strange alterations in the furniture.

The outside world obliged Hazel by being as gray and unpleasant as possible. Winter had seemed like such a new, bright thing just a week before. Now it felt eternal.

Mr. Lewis did call Hazel's mom, and on Friday morning she drove Hazel to school and the three of them sat in his office while he spoke of referrals and evaluations and partnerships and time-outs. Hazel was surprised that he did not mention sticker charts. She sat, her arms crossed, and stared out into the gray-coated world while her mother nodded and listened and asked questions. And then they were done, and Mr. Lewis promised a glorious, sparkly, partner-y future, and Hazel and her mom walked off into the waiting area.

Her mom was quiet and did not look at her. Her lips were pressed together and her eyes were dark. She stopped for a moment, her eyes on the big flower arrangement that sat on the table.

"They're fake," Hazel said.

Her mom rolled her eyes. "Of course they are." She glanced over to the office and then looked at Hazel seriously. "Are you okay?"

Hazel looked at the ground and shrugged. Wasn't the whole point that she wasn't okay? "They're going to figure out what's wrong with me."

Something flashed over her mother's face, and she

leaned down and put a hand on Hazel's shoulder. "Hazel," she said, voice firm and grave. "Listen to me. There is nothing wrong with you. Got it?"

Hazel nodded. She understood. They were plastic flowers of words—but they looked nice on the surface.

"Good."

Hazel walked back to her classroom through the hallways. They were empty, and it seemed like her steps should be echoing through them, a pronouncement that she was passing through. But her feet in her sneakers were silent, and Hazel moved through the hallways without making a mark, as if she was never there at all.

For once, the classroom door did not creak when she opened it, and no one turned to look at her when she slipped through. She crept across the room to her microscopically out-of-line desk and sat down silently in her seat, all without disturbing the air. Mrs. Jacobs kept talking, and everyone kept doing the things they were doing. Now she lacked weight, gravity, she was less than the air. No one noticed her at all.

Except one person.

Tyler had been doing this to her all week—staring at her like he wanted to gouge her with his eyes. It was getting a little tiring. And pointless. He had already won.

And now as she sat down she felt his eyes on her for a moment. At least it was confirmation that she was still there.

At the end of the day, Hazel gathered her things while everyone buzzed around her. She started to float out in the cloud of noise and energy created by people who affected the world, and was surprised to hear someone say her name.

"Hazel?"

It was Mrs. Jacobs. She braced herself.

"Are you all right?" The teacher was looking at her with concern in her eyes.

Hazel blinked. "Yes."

"Okay," said Mrs. Jacobs. "Okay."

Hazel floated onto the bus, sat down in her usual seat, and pulled out a book. When she felt a body sit next to her, she half wondered if its owner even knew there was someone already there. Until she realized who it was.

"What now?" she asked Tyler.

She looked at him with all the weight and gravity she could muster. But he did not look triumphant or mocking. His cheeks were dark. His eyes were serious.

"What is it?"

"It's Jack," he said, his voice low and strained. "I saw something."

She blinked. "What do you mean you saw something?"

"I mean I *saw* something." He looked around and then leaned in and whispered. "I don't think Jack's with his aunt."

Hazel wrapped her arms around her chest. "What do you mean?" she asked carefully.

"We were supposed to go sledding," Tyler said, looking around again. "And I was early. There was no one on the street, it was weird, and it was like I didn't want to go out either, like I had something else to do. But we had plans. So I went. And Jack was already there, at the top of the hill." He stopped and shook his head.

"Tyler," Hazel said. "What are you trying to tell me?"

"I know it sounds crazy, okay? But I'm not crazy. I'm not."

"Okay. I get it," she said, voice tight. "You're not crazy. Now, tell me!"

"He wasn't alone. There was a woman there. She was . . . she wasn't right. She was tall and weirdly thin. She wasn't real. She was all white and silver and made of snow . . . like an elf or a witch . . . like a movie."

She stared at him. "What are you talking about?"

"It's true, okay? She had a sled. It was huge and white and there were all these huge dogs, except I'm not sure they were dogs and—" He caught his breath and looked around the bus. "And he got in the sled and drove into the woods.

And I called after him, but . . ." He shook his head and looked away.

Hazel gaped. Did he know Adelaide somehow? Had she told him about the Snow Queen?

"This isn't funny," she said.

"I'm serious!"

"You're trying to trick me."

"I am *not*."

"You're lying. You're lying and I'm going to throw something at you every day for the rest of your life."

He gritted his teeth. "Hazel, stop being a psycho and listen, okay? I'm sorry I was mean. I'm sorry we didn't let you hang out with us. But you have to believe me."

"Why?"

"Because you're the only one who'll believe me. I mean"—he shrugged—"you know how you are. . . ."

He looked at her and she saw tears in his eyes, she saw that he was wrapped in heaviness, a blanket of snow. Like her.

"Somebody took Jack," she said. "Into the woods."

"Yes. That's what I'm trying to tell you."

"A woman in white on a sleigh. Like Narnia."

"What's Narnia?"

Hazel rolled her eyes. "Okay, then," she said, crossing her arms, "what happened before?"

"Before?" Tyler shook his head. "He was sledding."

"No," she said, talking over the thing that had wedged in her throat. "Before that. He changed. He was mean. He stopped being my friend. What happened?"

Tyler blinked at her. "I don't know, Hazel. I thought he'd finally figured out we were more fun."

Hazel closed her eyes and saw herself bashing Tyler on the head with all the pencil cases of the world.

She got off the bus and walked slowly home, Tyler's words buzzing in her head. It was absolutely crazy, what he had said. He was teasing her. He knew about the Snow Queen somehow. He was trying to get her to make a fool of herself. Because he knew what she was like. And then he would tell the whole school that Crazy Hazy believed Jack was kidnapped by a witch.

But then there was the way he looked, so serious, so shaken, like someone who had recently learned that the world was not at all what he thought it was.

Hazel walked into her house, nodded at her mother who was on the phone, and went straight to her room, where she set her backpack on the floor and lay down on the bed.

It was absolutely crazy, what he had said.

She looked at her shelves, filled with books in which the bad stuff that happened to people was caused by things like witches who lured people into the woods. In a weird way, the world seemed to make more sense that way. At least it always had to Hazel.

It was what she wanted to hear, what he had said. That it had nothing to do with her. That it was magic. That a witch had enchanted him and swept him off into the night. That she could still get him back.

Her eyes fell on the Joe Mauer baseball that was propped up on the shelf. He had given her something like his beating heart once, because she needed it, and because he knew she would keep it well.

And then something happened, something changed, and he was gone. And it might be true that he had just changed, that he didn't want to be her friend anymore, that he had grown out of her like a puffy purple jacket, that he had gone to stay with his elderly aunt Bernice. It was most likely true.

But what if it wasn't?

It might be true that something else had happened, something bad, something that flickered outside the boundaries of the things you could see. It might be true. Because who was Hazel to say what the world is really made of?

It might be true.

And if it was true, Hazel was the only one who could save him. Because, like Tyler said, she knew how she was. And because she was Jack's best friend. And that meant she would not give up on him, could not give up on him, without doing everything possible to save him.

It might be true.

It would not hurt, after all, to walk into the woods.

Hazel looked at the baseball and then exhaled. Tyler's face flashed in her mind. The pieces clicked together.

I believe there is magic in the woods, Uncle Martin had said.

What if there was?

Hazel's heart sped up. She sat up and looked around her room, then got down from the bed and opened her backpack and unloaded everything—all of the books and folders and notebooks—and hid them under the bed. She had to be prepared. She must carry things with her.

She got out a change of clothes and stuffed it into the backpack. She was tempted to bring another. It could be days. But she should travel light, she knew that much. And she could always wash her clothes in a stream. People did that kind of thing in books.

The two teddy bears, the orange kitten, the beat-up Grover she'd had since she was two, and the large purple hippopotamus on her bed eyed her as she moved. She remembered the compass her father had gotten her last Christmas as part of a junior adventurer's kit and she grabbed it, and then dug out the flashlight, the canteen, and the whistle from her bottom drawer. The kit had had a Swiss Army knife, but Jack broke it performing an emergency tracheotomy on the dinosaur rock at the park.

And then she found herself looking at the baseball again. It would be lucky, Jack had promised, for it was a baseball signed by Joe Mauer. She grabbed it and put it in the backpack.

She crept into the kitchen and pulled out some of the energy bars her mother alleged were food and filled up the canteen with water, then took a deep breath and went into the living room, where her mother was still on the phone.

Heart in throat, Hazel gave her a "do you have a minute" look.

"I'm sorry," her mother said into the phone, "could you hold on a second? . . . What is it, Hazel?"

"Um, I'm going to go to Mikaela's. We have a group project."

"Oh!" She cast a glance at the clock. "Look, if you wait a half hour, I can drive you."

"Oh, no. That's okay. It's not that cold."

Her mother nodded. "Remember, I have class tonight. I won't be home when you get home."

Hazel gulped. "Okay, Mom." And her mother nodded and turned back to the phone.

Hazel stood for a moment, looking at their living room.

It held a yellow couch that some long-dead cat had scratched up, a TV perched on a small cart, her mom's desk with a computer and all kinds of papers, and a row of shelves teeming with books. The walls were light blue, Hazel's favorite color. She'd helped her parents pick the paint four years ago, and her dad spilled a whole bucket of it on his shirt. You could trace his path through the house by the little drips that still lingered everywhere like breadcrumbs.

It was one of the few records of his ever living there. There used to be pictures of the family scattered around the living room, but her mom had packed them all away, and now the only record of Hazels-past was last year's school photo, preserving Hazel forever in long braids and a puffy green T-shirt that Jack thought made her look like a vegetable.

She stood so long that her mother gave her a questioning look, and she smiled as if everything was okay and put on her jacket.

"'Bye, Mom," Hazel whispered. She stood there for one beat. Two. And she went out the front door.

Hazel was trying so hard not to think, because if she thought about what she was doing she could never possibly do it. Instead she put one foot in front of the other, her sneakers crunching the snow, her socks absorbing the wet and cold and transmitting it up her legs. Already she'd made a mistake, but she could not risk going back for boots.

Anyway, how cold could it be in the woods at night, right?

Hazel trudged forward, down the long blocks to the park with the good sledding hill. She noticed among the footprints in the hard snow some tracks, like from a dragging sled, and she wondered if she was seeing the last record of Jack and when that record would melt away into nothing.

There were kids at the park, building snowmen, having snowball fights, barreling down Suicide Hill. Hazel walked as far around them as she could. She had a reason to be apart from them now. She climbed up the hill at the other side of the park, feeling the effort in her legs. The trees stood in front of her like sentries, and she could not tell whether they intended to welcome her or keep her out.

She stood looking at the line of trees that demarcated the woods as clearly as any doorway. Uncle Martin was right. She knew it at that moment. There were secrets, and there were witches in white, and somewhere there was Jack.

She wished he were with her now.

Hazel had read enough books to know that a line like this one is the line down which your life breaks in two. And you have to think very carefully about whether you want to cross it, because once you do it's very hard to get back to the world you left behind. And sometimes you break a barrier that no one knew existed, and then everything you knew before crossing the line is gone.

But sometimes you have a friend to rescue. And so you take a deep breath and then step over the line and into the darkness ahead.

Chapter Thirteen

SPLINTERS

Once upon a time, a demonlike creature with a forty-seven-syllable name made an enchanted mirror. The mirror shattered in the sky. The splinters took to the wind and scattered for hundreds of miles. When they fell to the earth, things began to change.

You might be swimming in a lake and come upon a spot that is cold and murky, and it feels like you have swum through a ghost. You might be walking in a grassy field and find a hard bit of dirt where nothing grows. You might be in a forest and find yourself in a patch of silence, as if no birds dare sing there. This is where the splinters fell.

Some went into the sand, and that sand became glass again, and that glass became all kinds of things, creating mischief beyond what even Mal could have imagined.

A woman got a new pair of eyeglasses. She left her husband the next day. She told him that she just needed to find herself, but it was a lie. "It was like I was seeing him through new eyes," she told a friend.

The president of a small corporation had a bathroom with a mirror installed just off his office. Within a week, he confessed to dumping chemicals in a nearby river. Within two weeks, he'd resigned and spent the rest of his days in a small cabin writing confessional poetry.

An astronomer looked through his new telescope into the stars one morning and then refused to ever look to the heavens again. When questioned, he said, "Some things we are better off not knowing.".

No one who tried on clothes in the third dressing room to the right of a certain department store ever bought anything. One observant employee suggested the room might be haunted. She was fired.

Every person who bought a particular model of television came to believe that TV shows had become particularly mean-spirited of late, and they all canceled their cable and took to other hobbies.

A certain shiny new subdivision featured windows made of the most state-of-the-art material. The neighbors peek out the window through closed curtains and keep to themselves.

Most of the splinters that fell were as tiny as dust. But there were a few larger pieces as well. The biggest one was about the size of your hand. It fell near the woods and a woman picked it up and carried it in with her. She dropped it when the wolves scared her, and it was picked up several days later by a girl who lived nearby. This girl did not need an enchanted mirror to show her that the world could be an ugly place, so to her it spoke the truth. She kept the mirror in her apron pocket, where it could be secret and safe.

A boy got a splinter in his eye, and his heart turned cold. Only two people noticed. One was a witch, and she took him for her own. The other was his best friend. And she went after him in ill-considered shoes, brave and completely unprepared.

PART TWO

Chapter Fourteen

INTO THE WOODS

Hazel stepped into the woods gingerly, expecting to land in a thick cushion of snow. So she stumbled when her foot went all the way to solid ground. It was not winter in the woods—at least in these woods.

She stood, rooted to the spot like the mammoth trees that surrounded her. Dark trunks traveled up into the distant sky, connecting this world to the one above. The distant roof was a tangle of budding branches. Decaying leaves clung fiercely to the floor among tiny green sprouts that aspired toward the world above. A cloud of mist hung in the sky like the aftereffects of a spell. The air was a tangible thing, rushing into Hazel's lungs as she breathed, touching her skin like a curious ghost. It carried with it the smell of old leaves and wide open sky. She was in the wood at the end of the world, or perhaps at the beginning.

She looked behind her, to remind herself of the place she came from, but it was gone. The wood stretched out in every direction. It was as if she had sprouted there.

She had stepped into the woods in the park and landed in an entirely different place. She knew this might happen. She'd been to Narnia, Wonderland, Hogwarts, Diction-opolis. She had tessered, fallen through the rabbit hole, crossed the ice bridge into the unknown world beyond. Hazel knew this world. And it should have made this easier.

But it did not.

Hazel shuddered. She couldn't get out even if she wanted to. But it didn't matter. She didn't want to get out, not now anyway. She had a job to do.

Hazel took a deep breath and was about step forward when some primal instinct made her turn her head to the left. And when she did she desperately wished she had a place to run to. For about ten yards away, next to one of the trees, was a large gray wolf.

Hazel froze. The wolf sat, erect and still, like a statue. His copper eyes gazed at her. She instinctively took a step backward and still he stared. Panic fused the circuits of her brain. Her breath stopped. She'd read once that if you ran into a bear in the woods you should avoid eye contact and you shouldn't run away, but all she knew about wolves was that you should never tell them how to find your grand-mother's house.

So Hazel lowered her eyes and took another step back, her skin crawling and her heart buzzing with fright. The wolf blinked, and in all the stillness it was as if he had leapt toward her. But he hadn't—he just stayed, regarding her, and his gaze was the world.

"Hi," she croaked.

Nothing.

"I'm just looking for my friend. I don't mean any harm."

Stare.

"Um, maybe you've seen him. His name's Jack. He's got freckles and a blue coat. He was with a woman on a sleigh, a witch or an elf? Dressed all in white . . ."

Blink.

"Well . . . I should be going, then." Hazel took one step back, then another, then, moving as slowly as possible, she turned around and began to walk away from the wolf.

It was all she could do not to take off and run as fast as she could. Her every muscle begged to be sprung. She wondered whether she would hear him as he approached, or if the next thing she knew would be his jaws on her neck, and then searing pain, and then nothing. But neither thing happened, and she carefully stole a look behind her to see the wolf still at his post, and still watching her.

She crept on for an eternity, one foot in front of the other, grateful for each and every breath. Finally, when she was well out of his sight, she leaned up against one of the trees and let out a great, shaking exhale.

The feeling of his eyes on her had not left her. It seemed like it would never go away, that she would spend the rest of her life feeling that predatory gaze.

She closed her eyes and gathered herself. *Find Jack.* That was all.

She looked around for some direction, some guidance, some place. There was a clearing up ahead, and it was, at least, a destination. Hazel moved softly toward it, conscious of advertising her presence with every step to all the watchful wolves of the woods. Not that everything was silent—the wind carried whisperings with it, a current of noise just underneath the airy quiet.

She listened, her ears learning how to work in this new world, and she could hear the sounds of birds chirping and trilling, and this was somehow comforting. Normal. There were birds in the woods, and they had things to sing of.

There was another noise in the wind, too, something that did not seem normal—at least not here. As Hazel continued to walk forward the sound clarified and she had to stop to take in what she was hearing.

Tick tock. Tick tock. Tick tock.

Hazel shook her head slightly at the strangeness of it, this once-ordinary sound that in the mist-filled forest felt like a mechanical menace. She moved toward the sound, the ticks marking out her steps, and she realized it was coming from the clearing. And then she saw why.

The clearing was about the size of the first floor of Hazel's house, and at the very center of it was a clock. It was a tall standing clock with a gold-trimmed face at the top like a head, supported by two steel beams. Three cylindrical weights hung down from behind the face, and a long pendulum swung back and forth over the ground. Behind the face you could see gears and cranks. It looked like a grandfather clock that had been skinned.

The clock was only about a foot taller than she was, and she stared up into its face as if to have a conversation. In the woods the sun was rising in the sky, but the iron hands pronounced the time as 5:43—probably about the time it was back in the real world. And that seemed the weirdest thing of all.

There was a squawking from above, followed by an odd croaking, and then some sort of throaty trilling, and Hazel looked up to see two big black birds perched on a branch behind her chattering to each other. The birds were the size of eagles and pitch-black, with long, hooked black beaks. They looked like crows, but puffier and shinier and much, much bigger.

Ravens. The word popped into Hazel's head. The bigger one turned its head toward her and looked back at her with beady black eyes, taking her in. Hazel shifted under its gaze, and it turned to its partner and croaked something. They chattered back and forth and Hazel understood that they were talking about her.

She took a deep breath. "I'm Hazel," she said. "I lost my friend. Do you know of a woman who looks like she's made out of snow?"

She felt like Alice, questioning caterpillars and grinning cats. *Would you tell me, please, which way I ought to go from here?*

The birds both turned their heads to look at her, and she stood in the middle of the clearing surrounded by tree giants while two dog-size maybe-ravens eyeballed her and a naked clock ticked on behind her like fate, and she felt quite small and quite real, and wondered what she thought she was doing and what she was going to do now.

And then one of the birds lifted its head slightly, focusing on a point somewhere beyond Hazel. She turned to follow its gaze and saw, leading out of the clearing, a small path.

She looked back at the birds. The smaller one croaked

something at her and flicked its head toward the path again, and then they turned back to each other. They were done with her.

Now, Hazel was not stupid. She knew that just because you see a piece of cake and a sign that says EAT ME doesn't mean you should actually do it. And just because two giant ravens point you in the direction of a path doesn't mean you should take it. But it was the only path she had.

Hazel crossed the clearing and stood in front of the path. It didn't look like anything out of the ordinary—just trodden dirt weaving around the trees. She took off her hat, mittens, scarf, and green jacket and put them in her backpack, then took out her compass, because it seemed like the thing to do. Her mom would be pleased. Hazel might have plunged into a mysterious fantasy woods after an evil witch with a pack of wolves at her disposal, but at least she'd brought a compass.

Hazel watched the face of the compass as the needle wavered slightly, as if afraid to make too firm a commitment. But it was pointing roughly the way she was heading. Hazel was going north. Her heart lifted a little. This might be a magic woods, but there was still a north here. It was a place, like any other. The compass would guide her to Jack, and then guide her home. Who needed breadcrumbs?

She had a compass. She had a direction. She had a

path. She knew where north was. So Hazel stepped on the path and headed forward.

Last year her class had taken a field trip through the woods in some state park or other. There was a guide who'd taught them how to spot poison ivy and look for water and find shelter, and Hazel had been too busy dreaming of centaurs to pay attention. The only thing she remembered was the guide passing out whistles and showing everyone how to blow three times for an emergency signal. The whole class practiced, again and again, while the guide whipped them up into a whistling frenzy. Hazel had been afraid they would scare off the centaurs.

She had the wilderness kit whistle in her backpack, and now could not imagine why. Because whatever the emergency was that might cause her to blow the whistle, there was no saying that whatever answered it wouldn't be far worse. It could be just the thing that allowed the Snow Queen's flying monkeys to find her.

Flying snow monkeys, probably.

The path led Hazel up an incline, and now she was moving along a ridge above the ravine. From somewhere down below she could hear a stream running. In another world she was on a field trip surrounded by all her old classmates, the guide was yammering on about potentially useful information while Hazel dreamt of magic.

It was then that she realized that the *tick tock* sound of the clock had never quieted—it was as if she was still standing next to it. She stopped for a moment and looked around, as if maybe she hadn't moved at all. But she had. And yet there was the sound: *Tick tock. Tick tock.*

Hazel stiffened. It made no sense—when she'd entered the woods she hadn't heard it at all, and it had gotten louder as she approached it. This is the way things worked. Now that it was in her ears, though, it seemed it would never go away.

She took a deep breath and moved on, her feet walking in rhythm with the clock. After some time, she came upon a fork in the path. Hazel looked from one side to the other and bit her lip, then consulted the compass. One was heading north and one eastward. Hazel was looking for a witch made of snow with a sleigh pulled by wolves. She would go north.

She walked on, consulting the compass when she needed to, always heading the direction it pointed. She was just thinking how odd it was that there was no one else in the woods when she felt a shaking on the ground and heard hoofbeats in the distance. They were coming toward her. Hazel stopped and looked behind her, but could see nothing.

She did not know these woods. She did not know the

rules. She did not know what manner of man patrolled the paths. All she knew was her job, and that was to get Jack and get out.

Clutching the precious compass, Hazel left the path and scurried into the trees to hide. She ducked behind a particularly wide one, and slowly peeked around to see who else was in the woods.

The hoofbeats approached and the ground beneath Hazel vibrated in response. Hazel moved her head out as far as she dared.

A man was on the path, riding a sturdy chestnut horse. The man was wearing a flannel shirt and a cloth hat. On one side of the horse hung a saddle bag and a long, old-fashioned ax.

Hazel understood. He was a woodsman. In a woods full of wolves there were woodsmen, too. Her heart eased.

The horse made a noise and stopped suddenly, pawing at the ground with its hoof. The woodsman whispered something to it and patted its flank. He reached into his saddlebag and began rummaging inside it. Something seemed to catch his attention then, and he looked around, eyes searching the trees. Hazel darted back, then wondered if she needed to. Maybe he could help her.

She peeked out again and the woodsman's posture had changed. He was erect, watchful. One hand held taut the reins of the horse, who was stomping agitatedly, and another clutched the handle of the ax.

Hazel felt the expectant hush in the air, like the trees were waiting for something. If she took a breath, the sound would shatter the silence. And then the horse let out a noise and the woodsman relaxed his grip on the ax and lifted the reins.

Her heart pounded. She'd asked a wolf and two ravens about the woman in white. It might be time to ask an actual person.

She gathered herself and stepped out from the tree. There, standing between her and the path, where a moment before had been nothing, was another wolf.

This one was bigger than the first, with a thick brown and black coat and creepy blue eyes. Hazel froze. She heard the sound of the horse stirring. The wolf was in the shadows, too far behind the man for him to see. And the creature had no interest in him at all—all its energy was fixed on her.

Hazel could scream. There was a wolf and a wood-cutter with an ax. This was the way the story went. She did not know how long it took a woodcutter to hear a yell, understand what it meant, unhook his ax, and swing—and how that compared to the time it took a wolf to cross the distance between desire and prey. The scream came out as a strangled, whispered thing, the sort that could barely bother the air.

She tried again. The word mustered inside her, air swirled around in her lungs, her vocal cords vibrated, her lips readied. "Wolf," Hazel said.

But the sound was no more than a breath.

And then some change on the wolf's face. A darkening. Its blue eyes flashed, and though he was some distance from her, she saw it like lightning. He lifted his lips and his face contorted into a snarl, revealing yellowing fangs. He growled, and only she heard it.

Hazel was nothing, nothing at all. She would disappear here in the woods and no one would even know she'd come.

The horse whinnied. The rider clucked. The hoofbeats started and began to travel off down the path. The wolf did not move, did not release her, did not ease his fangs. The horse and rider disappeared into the distance and still Hazel stood.

Finally the wolf relaxed, the cable that tied them together broke. Hazel eyed the wolf, who still stood in front of the path. And then slowly turned her head toward the woods behind her.

"I'm going to go over there now," she told the wolf.

He did not answer.

She willed herself forward. She took a step—and heard

a small plastic-y crunch. She stopped. The hand that had been clutched around the compass was empty. She picked up her foot and saw just underneath the cracked remnants of her guide to Jack. Her heart sank. Of course, it might still work, it might still point north, she might still be able to use it to get there and even back again.

She looked down at the compass for a moment, pictured herself bending down to pick it up. Her neck tingled. She turned to see the wolf pacing on the path now, back and forth like a sentry.

Then Hazel noticed something on the path, something that had definitely not been there before. She stared. There, in the middle of the path, was a pair of shoes. The woodsman must have dropped them.

They were not just any shoes. They were girl's shoes, for one, something close to the size of the battered sneakers on Hazel's feet. And they were beautiful, better than the sum all of the shoes Susan had in her closet—shiny slippers with a pile of long ribbons on top. And they were a bright, beckoning red.

They were dancing shoes—real ballet slippers, not just what Adelaide had, but the kind they have in books, the kind where you can wrap the ribbon around your ankles. They were shoes that called to Hazel's heart. They were full of promise, of leaps and pliés and the feeling of being lighter than air. They were not for the woods, but they were for everything after.

Hazel took a step toward the shoes and the path. And the wolf stopped. And stared. And bared his teeth.

He was taking those from her, too.

There was nothing she could do. So, leaving the cracked toy among the leaves and the shoes on the path, she turned around and headed into the trees.

Chapter Fifteen

SKINS

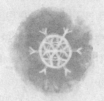

Hazel scooted forward quickly, though her heart still tried to tug her back. She didn't even know where she was going, or whether she could find her way back home, but the path belonged to the wolf now.

Maybe, when she had Jack, she could come back for the shoes.

The best she could do was move along the edge of the ravine. The path had been running parallel to it—logically it still would be—and at least that way she'd still be going in the direction the raven had told her to.

She trod along the unsteady ground, trying to move as soundlessly as possible. The sun was at its peak in the sky now. She'd been walking for at least half a day. Her body was wearing, and there was no sign of anything that would point her to Jack. She thought again of the woodsman, and what he might have told her, and hoped there were as many woodsmen here as wolves.

But she went on, following the ravine below, up a hill and then back down again, wondering if she was going in the right direction, or in any direction at all, accompanied all the while by the ticking of the great clock.

She came upon an area of flat ground, about the size of her school gym. And spread over much of it was the canopy of a tree that had a trunk the width of a minivan. This tree, unlike every other one she'd seen, still had its leaves—a massive cloud of green hanging low over the grassy land and supported by a mess of tangled branches. It looked like an entire world might live within those leaves.

Hazel could not help but stop and stare at it—this, the biggest tree in the world. There was flickering within the leaves, birds that made their universe inside the mammoth cloud of branches. She wondered if they even knew about the sky.

Her eyes traveled past the tree, and then her heart lifted. For, just when she needed it, the path had appeared again.

She moved toward the path, wondering at the mas-sive tree as she passed around it. And then she noticed the three women who sat at its base.

These women had oddly smooth features and eyes that were mostly pupils. They wore cloaks of a soft gray with hoods that framed their faces in shadow. They each had dark brown hair, dark skin, and deep brown eyes, so they looked like sisters to the tree behind them. A string of gray yarn stretched across them, and the last woman was working on a large wooden spinning wheel.

And as one all three turned to look at her.

"Oh, hi!" shouted the first. "Come here!" She motioned Hazel over with a cheerful wave. Hazel glanced toward the path, then took a few steps toward them.

"What's your name?" the woman asked brightly.

"Um"—Hazel pressed her shoe into the ground— "Hazel Anderson."

"Oh," said the first. "You don't look like an Anderson."

"That's rude," said the second.

"So sue me," said the first. "We get a lot of Andersons here," she added to Hazel, by way of explanation. "Now . . ." She bent down, and as the other two watched her, began rummaging in a small wooden box that lay at her feet. The woman picked up a handful of gray strings and sorted through them, and then looked at Hazel thoughtfully. "Has that always been your name?"

"I'm pretty sure that's rude, too," said the second.

Hazel felt herself flush. Her parents had never mentioned it. She had never asked. But it probably hadn't always been her name. Someone had called Baby-Who-Would-Be-Hazel something before her parents flew in on their rocket ship to get her, in the place where there was culture. There was the orphanage—she was there for months. Surely the nurses murmured something to her as they gave her a bottle and changed her diaper and placed her back in her crib. And somewhere there was a before-mother—and maybe a before-father, too. And maybe the before-mother never gave her an official name, maybe she never even held her, maybe she decided to give the baby up before it became something other than a red squalling it. But there must have been something in her head at some point—a wish, a whisper—some dream of a future with a daughter. There must have been a name.

"I don't know," Hazel said, shifting.

"You don't know your name?" breathed the first.

"No," said Hazel.

The first woman shook her head. "How do you expect to know who you are?"

She looked at Hazel like she expected an answer, but Hazel did not have one to give. The first woman sighed and rummaged through the threads some more. "Aha!" she said suddenly. "Lookee lookee, Cookies!" She picked a long gray string out of the box. It had a puff of wool attached at one end. She passed the string down, puff end first, and the three hooded women stared at it as if it were the most fascinating thing in the world.

"Is that me?" Hazel asked quietly.

"It is," said the first woman, raising her head.

"You're like the Fates."

"Somebody had to do it," said the second woman. "This is the sort of place where people want answers."

Hazel stared at the long, ordinary thing. "Does that mean you know what's going to happen?"

The third one held up the messy, unformed puff of wool and threw up her hands.

"Oh," Hazel said. She shifted. "Um, do you . . . can you see my name?"

"Nope," said the first, shrugging.

"Okay." Hazel looked down and began to dig her foot into the ground. And then she stopped. What was she doing? This wasn't about her. "Um," she interjected, raising her voice. "I lost my friend."

All three heads tilted sympathetically.

"That's sad," said the first woman.

"I'm so sorry," said the third.

The second woman looked intently at her portion of the string. "Oh! You're looking for your friend!"

"Yes," said Hazel, wrapping her arms around herself. Wasn't that what she'd said?

"Your *best* friend," the woman continued. "But wait!" She raised a hand. "He *changed*." She drew out the last word dramatically, and then turned to the others. "Isn't that like a man?"

The three women giggled.

The second one turned back to Hazel. "He changed. But you came into this dark place filled with mysteries, wonders, and terrors *beyond your imagination*"—she stuck her hand out, palm first, and swept it though the air dramatically—"to save him."

"Um"—Hazel blinked—"right."

"And to learn about yourself."

"No." Hazel shook her head. "I just want to save my friend. Please," she said, not trying to keep the desperation from her voice. "Do you know where he is?"

"I'm sure we can help you," said the woman in the middle. "But we need something from you."

"Something shiny," said the third one. The other two nodded.

Hazel looked at them to see if they were serious. They apparently were. She exhaled. "Um," she said, taking down her backpack. She had done her best to be prepared, but had not anticipated the crazy people. She pushed aside her jacket—which she was not giving up—and change of clothes, and then her hand settled on the flashlight.

"Will this work?" she asked, taking it out and turning it on. She shone the beam on the ground.

"Oh, yes!" exclaimed the third woman. Hazel walked it over to her, and she grabbed it eagerly and then sat there, flicking it on and off.

"What's your friend's name?" asked the first.

"Jack," Hazel said. "Jack Campbell."

"Coming up, Buttercup!" She bent down and began rifling through the box. She took out a clump of gray yarn and began to sort through it, and then frowned and picked up another clump. She shook her head and looked up. "Jack Campbell?"

"Yeah," said Hazel, a twinge of something in her stomach.

The woman shook her head. "I can't find his thread," she whispered to her colleagues.

Hazel's stomach dropped. "Does . . . that mean he's dead?" she asked.

"No," she said. "I would still have it."

"But"—Hazel looked frantically from one to the other— "what does it mean?"

"Wait," said the third woman, looking up suddenly. "How did you lose your friend, exactly?"

"He was taken. By a woman on a sleigh pulled by wolves."

The women all stiffened.

"Oh."

"Oh."

"Oh."

"Do you know who she is?" Hazel asked. "Do you know where she is?"

"You don't want to go there," said the third.

"Shhh!" the second said.

"We can't help you," said the first.

"Nope," said the second.

"They're right," said the third. "Go home."

"Wait," Hazel said. "What do you mean? Can't you tell me anything?"

They all shook their heads as one. Hazel stared at the women as if trying to pull information out of them with her eyes. And they all looked away.

They were supposed to help her. Why were they there, if not to help her?

Hazel stood there for a few more moments. She would not cry. "Well, thanks for your help," she said finally, and turned and walked to the path.

Hazel followed the path through the clearing and up a hill into the trees, heart burning the whole way. She did not understand what had passed. It was like they knew, when they couldn't find his string, what had happened to him. Something about the thought turned Hazel's stomach. Why wouldn't they tell her anything? Was the witch so scary they couldn't speak of her? All she'd been thinking of was rescuing Jack. It hadn't really occurred to her that she'd be rescuing him *from* someone.

And why wouldn't Jack have a string, anyway? He wasn't dead, they said it didn't mean he was dead. But Hazel knew that anyway—you know when a piece of yourself leaves the world, never to return.

Hazel had a string. This was a strange idea to get used to. She was a puffy, unformed mass of wool leaving something definite and fixed in her wake. Every step she took in the woods was one more bit of string left to time.

And time was passing. *Tick tock. Tick tock.* The sun was lower in the sky than it should be—she hadn't been in the clearing that long, but it looked like late afternoon now. It didn't make sense.

That wasn't the only thing. She reached the crest of the hill and heard the bubbling of the stream. She had met up with the ravine again—but it was on the wrong side.

Hazel looked around. Was she going in the wrong direction? That wasn't possible, was it? If she knew anything about anything, she would be able to look at the shadows the trees cast and know if she was going backward. But she hadn't been paying attention before. She never paid attention to the things she was supposed to. She never had to, before—there had always been Jack.

Somewhere, hours from here, a cracked Junior Explorer compass lay on the floor of the woods.

Her heart twinged. Her legs whined. Her body protested.

There was nothing to do. Hazel stepped off the path and plopped down behind a nearby tree. She rummaged through her bag, and her hand touched on the Joe Mauer baseball. A pang of missing Jack went through her. Then she pulled an energy bar and her canteen out of her backpack for some approximation of lunch. The energy bar tasted as good as she felt.

But Hazel still ate the whole thing, washing it down with water from the canteen. Then she sighed and looked around for some sign of anything. Something squeezed in her chest. She had no idea where she was or where she was going. And she was alone. No one ever has to do these things alone.

Usually, they at least have a friend with them.

Hazel wrapped her small arms around her small chest and looked around at the great trees. She kept her eyes level—she felt all of a sudden if she looked up and saw how far they reached into the sky she would disappear alto-gether.

And then her eye caught on a flash of something out of place. She squinted. About ten yards away, near the ravine, something white was tucked into the hollow of a tree.

Maybe it was something. Hazel needed something.

She grabbed her backpack and crept toward the tree, looking around carefully as she went.

It looked like a garment at first, a cast-off cloak made of small white feathers. It was tucked away in the hollow, as if someone had hidden it there. Hazel put her backpack down, grabbed a thick stick, and poked the mass. Nothing hap-pened, so she bent down carefully and placed her hand on it.

It was the softest thing she had felt in her life, and everything that was twisting inside of her stopped. As if there was no need for fear or loneliness when there was such softness in the world.

She picked up the feathery garment—it was surpris-ingly thick and heavy—and then yelped and dropped it. For attached was a long slender neck that supported a beautiful white head with a black mask and a bright orange beak.

It was a swan, but with no swan inside.

Hazel stared at the thing at her feet. A dead eye stared up at her. It had been alive once. It had been a swan and someone had taken it and killed it for this skin.

Hazel knew about this from fairy tales. There were people who could turn themselves into an animal by wrapping themselves in its skin. It had always seemed to Hazel like the most wonderful power—to be able to transform yourself into something else entirely.

Hazel looked around again and then picked up the skin and let it unfurl. The swan had been no ordinary bird—the skin belonged to a creature bigger than Hazel. It must have been magnificent.

Maybe she could do it. In the real world Hazel was an ordinary thing, a misshapen piece with no purpose. Maybe here she could be a swan. Maybe it had been left here, just for her. She could fly over the woods to rescue Jack. She could bear him on her back on the way home. She would alight just before the edge of the wood and unfurl herself. And then maybe she would hide the skin there, deep in the hollow of a tree, for when she needed to spread enormous white wings.

She held it up. The neck and head hung to the side, and Hazel tried to ignore the way her stomach turned looking at it. After all, she was not the one who'd killed the creature.

She felt naked as she began to wrap it around herself, like a bird plucked of its feathers—all goosebumpy skin and trembling bones and frail, sputtering heart.

And then the skin was around her and Hazel was

softness, she was warmth. The skin settled into her as if made for her.

But she was no swan. She had legs, she had arms, she had a swan neck dangling uselessly behind her. Of course it would never work, not on her. She didn't even know her name.

Hazel walked over to the edge of the ridge, thinking she might catch a glance of her reflection in the stream below. But it was too far away, and moving too quickly. It didn't matter. Hazel knew what she looked like. The skin was just a taunt, just one more thing she would never have. And she was still alone.

She tore the skin off and hurled it into the ravine.

Hazel watched as the beautiful, terrible thing fell into the water. It could not fly, it could not float, because all its swan-ness had been taken away. She stared down at the ravine, and then turned and walked slowly back to her backpack.

And a hand grabbed her arm.

"Where is it?" a voice hissed in her ear.

A woman was standing over her, her hand clutching Hazel's arm like a claw. The woman did not look right. Her skin was sickly yellow, and it hung oddly on her too-thin body, like someone hadn't gotten the size right. Big dark eyes popped out of a head that was a layer of skin away from being a skull. Nearly colorless hair hung in deadened strings over her shadowy, gaunt face.

Fear exploded in Hazel's stomach and she sucked in breath. She could not tell whether or not the woman was human or something else, but it didn't seem to matter, because the woman oozed blackness and rot. Hazel exhaled in a whimper, and the woman leaned into Hazel and sniffed her.

"My skin," she said again, her voice a parched rasp. "You touched it. I can smell it on you."

"I—" Hazel tried to back away, but the woman's grip on her arm tightened.

"Where is it?" she repeated.

"I—I don't know—"

"You think you can lie to me, you worthless thing? Who put you up to this? Were you going to sell it?"

"No—"

The woman's head tilted, and a cracked smile spread slowly across her yellowed face. "Did you think you could use it yourself?" She drew out the last word in a hiss. Hazel sucked in breath in little pathetic gasps. "Did you want to be a beautiful swan, you ugly little girl? Did you think you could fly?"

Her face was right up against Hazel's now, enough so that Hazel could smell the odor of decay that emanated from her. Hazel squirmed, trying desperately to wrench herself free. The woman's grasp tightened.

"You think I'm going to let you go? Is that what you think?" She pulled Hazel into her and clutched her against her chest. Hazel could feel the woman's body against her back, and it was all bone and rattling breath. "Tell me where it is," she whispered into Hazel's ear. "Now."

Hazel should have had a story ready. Something. Something to say that the woman would believe. This is what you were supposed to do now, come up with a clever story. But her mind was nothing but fear and pain.

She could only whimper, "I'm sorry."

"I see," the woman said, running a cold finger down Hazel's cheek. "Actions have consequences, little girl."

And then there was pain. Stinging, and then searing. The woman had stuck a nail into Hazel's cheek, and it was like a talon. She dragged her finger down, splitting the skin on Hazel's face. It traveled down her cheek to her neck.

"Did you want to be beautiful?" she hissed. "Is that what you wanted?" She moved her hand to Hazel's wrist and lifted her arm above her head, twisting it in a way it was absolutely not supposed to go. Hazel yelped, and tears sprung to her eyes.

"Now you're coming with me."

Hazel was bent over, trying to un-contort her arm, her

body alive with panic. She could not get away. She had to get away. Her cheek was hot and wet and stinging with pain. She needed something, anything.

"Wait," Hazel said, or something very like that. "I'll take you to it!"

The woman loosed her grip slightly and Hazel lunged for the nearest thing—which turned out to be the arm strap of her backpack. She hurled the backpack up at her attacker, using all the force of her body.

Her wrist exploded in pain. The backpack slammed into the woman's skull face and she stumbled backwards.

Clutching the backpack by the strap, Hazel took off in a run, darting through the trees, leaping over roots and clumps. She dared not look back, she just ran.

And then her foot hit something and she went flying into the dirt. Her hands skidded on the ground and her knee bumped up against a rock, tearing the leg of her jeans. Hands stinging, knee throbbing, she sprang back up again.

She could not hear anything but the sounds of her own breath, heart, and blood—all so loud that she wouldn't have heard a semitruck behind her.

Anyway, the woman had come upon her silently before, with nothing but the squeezing of her claw hand to announce her presence. It was not something Hazel wanted to experience again.

And so when the hand landed on her arm, she shrieked. But it wasn't a claw hand at all. A teenage boy was leaning out from one of the trees, arm outstretched. He grabbed her and pulled her behind the tree, then put his arm around her and whispered, "Come with me."

Chapter Sixteen

THE BIRDKEEPER

The boy guided her forward, moving quickly in and out of the trees. He kept looking behind and then urging her onward.

She had no business trusting this boy. Except he was getting her away from the swan lady, and that's all she cared about in the entire world.

Her leg hurt as she ran, and she could feel fresh blood on her face. Her hands still stung, and her knee was raw. But still she ran.

And then suddenly they came upon a small wood cabin. There was an ax leaning against the front wall and a pile of logs off to the right. The boy stopped and looked wildly around, then skipped up to the door, unlocked it, and motioned to Hazel to go inside.

"Wait in there," he whispered.

She looked from him to the door.

"Please," he said. "I won't hurt you. But she's coming."

And she will hurt you, Hazel finished silently. She ran up the step and into the cabin.

The boy did not come in. He closed the door behind her, and in a blink of an eye she heard the sound of wood being chopped.

Hazel knew she should be wary, knew she shouldn't trust a boy in the woods, but she had no wariness left. She collapsed in a heap on the floor.

She lay there, shaking. It was all too much, the monstrous woman and the monstrous fear. She could feel the woman's hand squeezing her, her nail in her cheek. Hazel was such a small, breakable thing.

She squeezed her eyes shut. For a moment, she imagined she was home in her own bed, the hum of her mom talking on the phone in the background. For once Hazel was fantasizing about the real world.

She inhaled and opened her eyes. Wherever she might want to be, she was here. She pushed herself up and eyed her surroundings. She was in a one-room cabin that was about the size of her classroom. There was a fireplace built into one wall, and above it hung two pots. A few shelves lined with jars of food hung next to it. There was a small bed against the other wall with a heavy blanket and a pillow, and a trunk at the foot. Near the fireplace sat a wooden table with a lantern and one chair. This was not someone who had a lot of visitors.

There were three strange things about the cabin. The first was the entire back wall, which was taken over by book-lined bookshelves, like a very rustic library. Except the books were not the musty, cloth-bound kind with gold lettering, but books like you might find at any bookstore now, like he'd just waltzed over to his neighborhood bookseller—or ordered UPS. The second was the rifle that hung above the doorway. It made Hazel's stomach wary just to look at it. And the third was the strangest thing of all.

Perched on a small table in front of the bookshelves in the back of the room was an ornate gold birdcage with its door open. And inside that cage was a small bird, like none Hazel had ever seen, as gleaming white as the feathers of the swanskin. The bird was about the size of a small robin, and from inside the gold cage it seemed to glow.

Hazel took a step toward the bird, mesmerized.

Then, the sound of voices from outside. She froze. Everything inside of her seized up, as if the claw hands were squeezing down on her right now. Hazel swallowed down the urge to vomit.

Making herself as small as she could, she crept over to the window to the left of the door. The shutters were closed, so she crouched underneath and listened, clutching her backpack in her hands.

Yes, it was the witch. Hazel could hear the rasping voice as if the woman was whispering to her heart. She couldn't make out what she was saying, but it hardly mattered.

And then the boy's voice. "No, I haven't."

Evil rasping.

"Mmm. I've been out here all day chopping wood. I'd have seen anyone come by."

More evil.

"I will. I will. Of course."

And then quiet, followed by the sound of wood chopping. Hazel pressed herself against the wall, barely able to breathe. She would not move, lest any disturbance in the air bring the woman back.

Hazel did not know how long she crouched there, while the bird skittered about the cage and outside the boy chopped wood. She just stayed, a puff of wool frozen in time.

And then the door opened and the boy burst in. "It's all right now," he said, hands out. "I don't think she's coming back."

The boy tilted his head, trying to reassure her with wide, gentle eyes. Hazel blinked up at him. He looked high school age, fifteen or so. He had a thicket of dark hair and wore a worn flannel shirt, rough brown canvas pants, and heavy black boots. His tan face was boyish, and there was no sign of stubble on his chin. He was too young to live in a house with just one bed.

Hazel could not speak, could not do anything but shake her head slowly.

"You need help," he said, his whole body cautious. "You're bleeding."

Hazel put her hand to her face and winced. Her hand came back red and sticky. Her stomach churned.

"It'll be okay," he said, reading her face. "It'll keep bleeding unless I put something on it, though. Is that all right?"

She nodded. He went over to the kitchen area and began poking around on the shelves. He got down a small brown bottle and a towel, which he brought over to her. "I'm going to clean this, okay?"

Hazel nodded again. The boy put some light yellow fluid on the towel and touched it gently to her cheek. Hazel had a flash of a memory—Jack's mom standing in front of her on some long-ago summer day, gently putting peroxide on a badly skinned knee, wincing along with Hazel.

"My name is Ben," he said, dabbing at her cheek. "By the way." He eyed her, but she had nothing to say. He lowered his voice. "Did you, um, do something with her swanskin?"

She nodded slowly.

He blew air out of his cheeks. "That was brave."

It wasn't, really.

"That'll stop bleeding now," he said, taking the rag away and stepping back. "It's going to leave a pretty good scar," he added. "I'm sorry. And, um . . . your clothes . . ."

She looked down. There was blood down the front of her sweater and smeared on one of the sleeves. She must have wiped her hand on her jeans at some point, because there were bloodstains there. The left leg of her jeans was ripped from the knee to her calf, and her knee was skinned underneath.

"I have more," Hazel said quietly, nodding to her backpack.

"Good," he said. "You don't want to walk around here with blood on you."

Hazel's stomach tightened. It didn't sound like it was just a laundry issue. "The wolves?" she asked.

He gave a grim smile. "It's not the wolves you have to worry about."

That was easy for him to say. "I don't understand this place," she said in a low voice.

He blew out air. "Then you're far ahead of everyone else."

She looked at him.

"You can't understand it. People think there should

be rules, or order. And sometimes when they can't find it they . . ." He waved a hand in the air. "Well, you met one of them."

Hazel looked down.

"I knew her, before," he added, settling himself into the wooden chair. "She was really beautiful once."

"Oh." That must have been a long time ago. "What happened?"

"She . . . wanted something she shouldn't want. There are costs for that kind of thing."

"I don't understand."

"You can't just kill a swan and wrap yourself in its skin, you know. It takes something from you. In her case it took the thing that she wanted most."

Hazel leaned forward. "What was that?"

"Beauty."

Hazel's hand traveled up to her face. She touched her wound lightly, tracing it from her cheekbone all the way down to her jaw. It throbbed at the barest touch. This was not supposed to happen.

"Um . . ." Ben clasped his hands together and leaned toward her. "May I ask what you're doing here?"

Hazel looked at the floor. It didn't seem like she was doing anything but spinning wool into gray thread.

"You should get out," he continued gently. "This woods

is no place for girls."

"I can't," Hazel whispered.

He sighed. "I know. It feels that way. You lost someone."

Hazel eyed him and nodded. "I lost my friend. How did you know?"

"Well . . . you're here, aren't you?"

She didn't understand. "Does everybody come here after somebody else?"

He looked at her a moment. "Oh," he said finally. "Oh, I see. You literally lost your friend? Here?"

"Yes. What did you mean?"

He shook his head. "Never mind. What happened to your friend?"

Hazel sat up. "He was taken. By a woman in a white sled. She wears white furs and doesn't look human. Do you know who she is?"

He sat back. "You mean the white witch," he said slowly.

A chill ran through her body. "The white witch?" she breathed. "Like Narnia?"

"No," he said, his voice quiet. "Narnia is like her."

Hazel's heart sped up. "Well, she took my friend," she said. "What does she want with him? Will she hurt him?"

Ben gazed at her for a moment. He seemed about to say something, and then stopped. "I don't think you should go after him," he said finally.

Hazel straightened. "What do you mean?"

"I think you should go home."

"No! I have to save him! She took him!"

"Look," he said, his voice gentle. "It might be that he doesn't want saving."

"Of course he does!"

"I'm sorry. It's just . . . the white witch . . . She wouldn't have taken him if he didn't want to go."

Hazel gaped. "What? Why would he want to go with her?"

"Look . . . I don't know. But you shouldn't go. People who go looking for her don't come back."

"I have to go!" Tears filled her eyes again. "I have to try to save him." Her voice was a trapped bird.

Ben looked at her and sighed. "Okay. Okay. I understand."

Silence settled in between them. Hazel blinked away her tears and tried to calm the thing inside her. She could feel Ben's eyes on her, and she tried to still herself, to seem very much like a girl who was not afraid.

"So, um," she said, trying to fill the air with something else. "Are you . . . from here?"

He let out a little laugh. "I'm from New Jersey. My sister and I . . . we ran away. Our father . . . " He shrugged. "I needed to get her out of there. There was a woods about a mile away from our house, and we were going to hide there for a night and then get a bus."

"Oh," Hazel said, looking down. There was no sign here of a sister.

"And of course the woods we entered weren't the ones we ended up in. We wandered around for a while, but, you know, I was just so happy to be somewhere else . . . I thought it would be better." He paused. "Well, Alice—that's my sister—she ate something she shouldn't have. At least that's what they told us. She got really sick. And this couple found us and they brought us to their cottage and took care of us. They were like real parents, you know? The kind you think you should have? And they sent me out to get some medicine, and when I came back . . . "

"What?" Hazel whispered.

"They said she'd run away. But I saw the bird and I knew. . . ." He glanced at the gold cage behind him. "It's just like her. And you always know your sister."

Hazel stared. "That's Alice?" she whispered.

He nodded.

She looked at the white bird in the back of the room. It didn't belong here. It didn't belong anywhere. But it was the most beautiful bird she'd ever seen.

"They tried to get rid of me," he continued. "Told me to go after her. But I came back at night and got her."

"I don't understand," Hazel said, her voice squeezed. "Why would anyone do that?"

He shrugged. "They wanted to keep her, I guess. The woods does funny things to people." He let out a small bitter laugh. "Anyway, I got what I wanted, right? No one will ever find us in here. And she"—he looked over at the bird—"no one's hurt her."

Hazel could not quite read his voice. He sounded half bitter, half serious. Her mind flashed to the Snow Queen, to the fairy tale she and Adelaide had told. That witch put kids into snow globes. *Why would they want to stay?* Adelaide had wondered.

"Can't you go anywhere? Other family or friends or . . ."

He shook his head. "There's no one. Not anymore. And, anyway, she's not from that world anymore. She's a creation of this place. I'm not sure she could . . . you know . . . *be* outside of these woods."

"Oh." Hazel hugged her knees and looked at the ground.

"I swore I'd protect her. And that's what I'm going to do. They'll come back, looking for her. That's what that's for." He nodded to the gun on the wall.

Hazel could not look at him.

"We're okay," he said, reading her face. "I read to her. She likes it. It's not hard to get things here. We don't usually have visitors, though." He allowed himself a half smile, but then his face turned dark again. "I understand why you have to go. Just . . . be careful. The witch is seductive. She will offer you things that seem good. You go, you find your friend, and get out of there. And get out of the woods as fast as you can. The woods do not mean you well."

"But I'm not doing anything wrong. I'm just trying to rescue Jack. That's good."

He eyed her. "I know. And that should matter. But it doesn't."

"Do you know where she is?"

"Follow the cold," he said. "It's that simple."

Follow the cold, Hazel said to herself. In her mind she was back on the path, heading north, and now she realized there had been something tugging at her, so gently it was barely a whisper. But it was there, and had been there the whole time, beckoning her forward. Follow the cold.

"Do you know how she'd keep him?" she asked. "Do you think he's locked up somewhere? How do I rescue him?"

He gave her a sad look. "I don't know. I don't know if any-one's ever done it before. I'm sorry. I wish I could help you."

"It's okay," Hazel said, though she wished he could help her, too.

"But I can tell you this," he continued. "The white witch doesn't feel things the way we do, do you understand? She's all ice. That is her whole point."

A palace of ice and a heart to match. "I don't understand. Why would people go looking for her? Why would they want to go with her?"

Ben sat back. He looked at Hazel searchingly, sadly. His shoulders rose and fell. "Sometimes," he said slowly, "it seems like it would be easier to give yourself to the ice."

Hazel's heart tightened. She got up. "I have to go," she said, looking as brave as she could.

"She was your age, you know. My sister." His eyes traveled to the cage, and then back to Hazel. "I wish I could go with you. But I can't leave her. She doesn't really know how to be a bird. I'm sorry. Promise me you won't mention us to anyone."

"I promise."

"Don't trust anyone. Stick to yourself. This place drives people to do strange things."

"I will."

"Follow the cold, but don't lose yourself to it, understand?"

"Okay."

He gazed at her, and then shook his head. "Look. I'm always here. If you need me . . . if something happens . . . you signal me, okay? If you're in the woods, I'll hear you. You can yell, or . . ." He looked around the cabin.

"I have a whistle," she said.

"Good. You just blow on it. It doesn't matter how far away you are. As long as you're in the woods, I'll hear you and I'll come for you, okay?"

"Okay," Hazel said. It didn't really make sense, but she believed him. This place was seeming less and less like a place every moment.

"And . . . remember. People who come here looking for things . . . they don't usually find what they want."

"I have to try to save my friend," she said.

"I understand," he said.

"I just want him back. That's all."

"I know. I hope it works."

Ben stepped out of the cabin so she could change, and Hazel got out the extra pair of jeans and the shirt that she'd brought. She folded up her bloody clothes on the wooden chair and let Ben back in. He said he would take her clothes and bury them, somewhere far away.

He refilled her water canteen, pointed her in the direction of the path, and told her again to be careful, eyes full of brotherliness. As Hazel left the small wood cabin, the small white bird began to sing, calling her back.

Chapter Seventeen

THE MARKETPLACE

Hazel walked through the trees toward the path, hearing the birdsong in her head. She wondered if the bird remembered anything of her life before, if she wanted to tell her brother things, if she dreamed of having two legs and running. Or did she just think about birdseed and wonder at that funny boy who read her books?

Ben was just a few years older than Hazel, and he was stuck here. He and his sister were all long gray string now.

A few days ago she would have found this story so beautiful. It was the sort of story your mother told you before she tucked you in at night, and you would sigh and think of the steadfast birdkeeper and his bird sister and the marvelous tragedy of it all. It would have been beautiful, as a story.

Hazel would have gone to sleep confident that if she were a bird, Jack would be her keeper, that they would spend their days in a small cabin tucked in the fairy-tale woods, and no one would ever tell them they needed to face reality. There was a time when this was true, but maybe not anymore. And maybe she wouldn't want him to anyway. Jack would have a big puff of wool left, and she could learn to be a bird.

Hazel didn't know what the right thing was. What are you supposed to do when something like that happens? Do you hold on or let go?

It didn't matter, though. Hazel was here, in this place where people did not mean her well. And she was on her own. No one even knew where she was. And if someone decided to turn her into a bird, there would be no one to look after her. She'd have to figure it out by herself.

Hazel stepped back on the path, but kept to the side. And she walked on.

She found herself reacting to every murmur of the wind—each and every one a potential footfall of someone coming toward her. There were witches in the woods, they stole beauty from swans and then rotted from the inside. There were couples who wanted to turn girls into pretty little birds. The woods does strange things to people.

Hazel was exhausted. Her wounds throbbed. Her

muscles felt like warm Play-Doh. She wanted nothing more than to curl up on a pile of leaves and rest, just for a few hours.

And the cold was there, too. It called her forward, whispering promises at her that it would not keep. Hazel's skin prickled underneath her shirt. She stopped and got out her jacket from her backpack. She saw the whistle at the bottom of the bag and tucked it into her jacket pocket where she could get it quickly if she needed it. At least she wasn't alone anymore. In some way.

Ahead of her, somewhere, was the white witch, who had a palace of ice with a heart to match. The Fates were afraid of her. Ben tried to warn her away. Hazel was supposed to defeat her, somehow—though she could not even function in the real world. What was she against a witch? She couldn't even deal with fifth-grade boys. All Hazel could do was try not to think about what lay ahead, to numb herself a little bit.

She ate another energy bar, and she no longer cared what it tasted like. She had two left. She should have asked Ben for some food. She should have rested there for the night. She should have thought.

The sky was darkening. It was going to be night soon, and Hazel realized that a wood-night is nothing like a city-night, that the darkness would have nothing to temper it, that unchecked by any light source anywhere it would swirl around her and squeeze her. And she had no flashlight. She had given it up because it was a shiny thing and she was hoping there were answers in a piece of string.

It had been evening when she crossed into the woods from the park. It would have been impenetrably dark within hours. What had she been thinking?

She put her hand on the whistle in her pocket. Ben would come. She could go back to his cabin and rest for the night. That would be the smart thing to do.

But she did not want to go backward. She was supposed to get Jack. That was all.

She could just walk a little more.

And so she did. She walked onward for another hour into the cold and dusk. *Tick tock. Tick tock.*

And then she felt a presence, something in the shadows, something all too familiar. She was not alone. She crept onward, her muscles tense, looking carefully around for her company.

And there. In the dark shadows a few yards off the path, two wolves. These were small and lean, and they paced back and forth in the trees, watching her carefully. Hazel gulped and kept moving forward, conscious of the eyes that stayed on her.

Her hand went to the whistle in her pocket. Ben. She

could use it, she could call him and he would come. But would he be fast enough?

Then she saw a glow touching the sky up ahead, and Hazel relaxed her hand and quickened her steps. She rounded a bend in the path and saw her salvation. There was a valley, just below, and in it a little village. It strad-dled a small, swift-moving river spanned by a little stone bridge. The houses were small, made of white stucco and dark wooden beams and thick thatched roofs. She could see people in cloaks riding horses and milling around the stone streets.

And then, on the other side of the path, two more wolves appeared. One sat down on its haunches just a few feet from her. The other walked parallel to her—a feral shadow.

Hazel looked at the ground and hurried her steps, try-ing to pretend she was not about to burst apart with fear. Her hand flew to the whistle again, as if that itself could protect her. When she looked up she saw that one more wolf had joined the group to her right. And that up ahead of her was a great wooden fence.

There was a gate in the fence, and Hazel rushed to it and knocked. A moment passed while her heart threatened to explode. And then the gate opened a crack.

A tall, dark woman in a cloak peered through the crack,

and when she saw Hazel her face changed. "Come in," she said. "Hurry."

The woman motioned her in. Hazel stepped forward, shooting a glance behind her as she went. Nine wolves were on the path behind her, all pacing restlessly, all watching her as she crossed through the gate. Hazel stared at them as the gate closed behind her.

"What are you doing out there at night?" the guard asked.

"I was looking for a place to rest," she said.

"Well, you found it. Good thing, too. The wolves are gathering. Don't worry, the fence keeps them out of here."

Hazel exhaled. "Good," she said. Her eyes traveled up to the guard, who was looking at her face with a curious expression. Hazel's hand flew up to her gashed cheek. The wound was thick and long and warm. She could only imagine how she must look.

"That looks pretty nasty," the guard said. "Something got you?"

Hazel nodded.

"Well, the market's on," she said. "As always. You can find whatever you're looking for there."

"Oh, I'm not . . . I lost my friend. I'm looking for him."

Her brow darkened. "What does she look like? Is she blond?"

"He," Hazel corrected. "He has brown hair."

"He? Oh." Something passed over the woman's face. "The princess is saving the knight, eh?"

Hazel shifted. "I guess."

"I hope the knight doesn't mind." She let out a laugh that sounded like it could cut something.

"Um," said Hazel. "Do you know the white witch?" She might as well ask.

The guard stiffened, and looked around. "You're new here, huh?" she asked, her voice lowered.

"Yes," Hazel said. Something began to gnaw on her heart.

"And you're . . . looking for her?"

"Yes."

"I see." The guard glanced at the ground. "Most people don't admit that, they just go."

Hazel's heart sped up. "What do you know about her? How do I defeat her?"

"Defeat her? That's what you want?"

Hazel did her best to look very brave. "Yes! She has my friend."

"I see. Look, kid. You can't defeat her. She's never going to go away."

"What do you mean?"

"I mean she's always waiting there, at the end of this

place. All you can do is pretend she's not there. That's what most people here do."

Hazel looked up at the guard, whose face was rueful and whose body seemed cloaked by more than wool. She was too tired to make sense of this senselessness. So she thanked her and walked past her, into the village.

Hazel walked down the hill to the marketplace. She didn't know what she was looking for, exactly—some available shelter she could crawl into, some Hobbit inn that took energy bars as payment. It did not matter, as long as there was a place to sleep.

But when she arrived at the market, she forgot her fatigue and simply stared at the scene before her. The marketplace was a cobblestone square about half a block wide surrounded by little shops, all cast aglow with torches. Even at night the square was thrumming with people. Hazel felt something unknot in her as she moved toward all of them. There was solace in company. At least right now. Hazel was tired of being alone.

She would have expected to stand out in the crowd here, with her backpack and jeans and shiny green jacket—not to mention her dark skin and hair. And there were plenty of people who looked like they'd dressed up for the Renaissance Festival, with wool cloaks and tall leather boots. But she saw a man in all black leather, another in a trench coat and fedora, a woman in jeans and a bright-red peacoat. And they weren't all white and European looking either—she saw African faces, Asian, Hispanic. It seemed like people had come from everywhere. For once, Hazel fit right in.

The noise of the market felt odd in Hazel's ears after all that quiet. There were merchants advertising their wares, people shouting, strains of music competing for attention. And there was a general hum of activity and humanity. The air carried with it the smell of smoke, cooking meat, and horse poop.

Near her, a skinny man in old jeans and a battered army jacket was playing the saxophone. A large yellow dog was curled up next to his legs, and next to it was an open instrument case. The man looked like someone you'd see on the street downtown, except instead of bills and coins in the instrument case, people had dropped little vials of colored powders and liquids.

There were other performers, too. Hazel saw a juggler off in one corner. There was a crowd around a woman who stood on a barrel—she seemed to be telling a story or giving a speech. And off in one corner there was a girl a few years older than Hazel, dancing.

Hazel moved into the crowd, checking out the merchants and their carts. There were things you might expect—produce and meats, tools, bolts of cloth, handmade jewelry. But there were odd carts, too. Hazel approached one that was covered in identical tiny glass jars. She stared into them, at the little odd blotches inside, until she realized each had a tiny clump of different kinds of human hair. There was a cart of books, as clean and modern as the ones on Ben's shelves. There was one that had dozens of little brass clockwork animals.

"I can make that scar go away," one of the merchants called to Hazel. She was two carts away, but Hazel's wound was apparently that noticeable.

Something flickered in Hazel's heart, and she tried to ignore it. This was not the time to be dealing with her scars. She turned and walked away, pretending like she wasn't interested at all.

She found herself at the edge of the row, in front of a small cart filled with vials of different-colored liquid. Behind it was a small white-haired woman in a flowered housedress. The woman smiled when she saw Hazel, and leaned toward her. "I have potions for you," she whispered.

The woman's eyes twinkled like a grandmother who'd announced she'd made cookies. Hazel could not help but look. Maybe there would be something she could use— something to put the white witch to sleep, or maybe a luck potion. Something. She had no payment, of course—unless the old woman was a Joe Mauer fan.

"What do you have?" Hazel asked.

"Mine are the best, you can ask anyone. I specialize, see? This row is for people, over here is events, and this row is for time. I can brew these for you if you're looking for something particular, but that's extra."

Hazel blinked. "A potion for . . . events or time?"

"For forgetting," the woman said, as if this was obvious.

"Oh," said Hazel. "I was looking for, like, a luck potion?"

"Oh," said the woman, like she had specially made chocolate chip and Hazel asked for oatmeal. "You won't find anything like that here."

"I guess I'm okay then."

"Are you sure?" The woman looked at her appraisingly.

"Yes," Hazel said, moving away.

What was she doing? She had no business looking for magic potions. She needed to sleep, and then she needed to find Jack. She was so tired that she was ready to curl up, right there in the marketplace, and let all the potion-seekers step over her. Her eyes traveled around the marketplace, looking for some idea of where to go. And then she saw someone who looked familiar.

Hazel walked over to where the performers were, past the saxophonist and the orator. At the very edge of the square was the dancing girl, and standing a few feet away was the woodsman Hazel had seen earlier that day.

Hazel went over to join the small group watching the dancer. Just then, a woman broke away from the group, shaking her head. The woodsman turned his head to watch her go. His eyes fell on Hazel.

"Some people just don't like ballet," he said, smiling.

His brown eyes were kind, just like a woodsman's should be. He looked a little like Jack's dad—he even had the same lines under his eyes—and the thought softened Hazel's heart. She gave him a little smile.

Her eyes went to the dancing girl. She was beautiful, with blond hair and big green eyes. She moved like the most elegant ballerina, like she could fly if she set her mind to it. There was no music, but it didn't seem to matter. The way she moved, Hazel heard the yearning of strings.

And then Hazel gasped. On the girl's feet were the red shoes.

She couldn't believe it. Someone had left them in the road and the girl had found them. They were magic. Hazel knew that when she saw them. And if she had picked up the shoes, she could dance like that.

"She's very good, isn't she?" the woodsman asked.

Hazel nodded, eyes on the shoes.

"My daughter was a dancer. She was very good, too."

"Oh." Hazel shot him a glance. She did not know whether he was using the past tense because his daughter no longer danced or because he no longer had a daughter, and she feared the answer.

"She gave herself up to it. Sometimes people get so focused on things they don't see the world around them. That's what I'm trying to tell people. It isn't easy."

Hazel nodded, though she didn't know what he was talking about. She was very tired. She needed to ask him for advice, that's why she'd come over.

"Do you like her shoes?" he asked suddenly.

Hazel nodded.

"Everyone does," he said, sounding a little sad.

Hazel was confused. Didn't he leave them? She watched the girl dance, bending and stretching and leaping. She noticed that there was sweat on her face and her expression was not of beauty or elation but something like pain.

"She looks tired," Hazel said. Though maybe she was projecting.

"She's been dancing a long time," said the woodsman. "This is what happens."

Hazel cast another glance at him. It was on the tip of her tongue to ask him for help, because he would surely take pity on a young girl who needed it—and take out any wolves she met along the way. But something stopped her.

"Is she okay?" Hazel asked.

"She will be," he said.

She wasn't sure she believed him. There was something weird going on. But she was so tired. Her head was fog. She wasn't thinking clearly, that was all. So she nodded good-bye to the woodsman, and with one last glance at the dancing girl, headed back into the company of the crowd.

Chapter Eighteen

TEMPTATIONS

As soon as she stepped back into the market, she felt a tap on her shoulder. Hazel whirled around to see a slim, slight man in a long black coat with two rows of shiny buttons down the front. He had a swoosh of black hair and a thin, pale face. He looked like he might have been blown in by the wind. His eyes reminded her of the bad guy Jack had showed her that day in the shrieking shack.

"Hello, young lady," he said in an accent thick with the forest. He motioned to the cart behind him. It was lined with vials of fluid and packets with different color powders, and standing in the center watching over it all was one mean-looking chicken. "May I interest you in a potion?"

What was it with this place and potions? She politely

refused, the same way she shrugged off the people trying to sell hair products at the mall. It was not forgetting that she needed.

"Oh," he said, luring her back with his voice. "I have all kinds of potions. I have the rare ones. I can give you your heart's desire." He took a step forward and studied her. "I can tell there is something you want. I know these things." He leaned over her, eyes penetrating her defenses, and whispered, "What does your heart yearn for?"

The way he asked it was like he was speaking directly to her heart, as if she was not even participating in the conversation. And the answer flew out of her mouth. "I want my friend back."

A slow grin spread across the man's face. "I see," he said. "Now—and please don't call me presumptuous—may I assume this was no ordinary friend?"

The marketplace bustled in the background, but it seemed to be distant somehow, as if Hazel and this man were the only true things in the world. It was like they were in their own pocket of air.

"No," Hazel said. "He's not."

"You feel like you are nothing without him. He made you feel worthwhile, and then took it away."

Hazel could not speak.

"That's what I thought," the man said. "I understand.

I've got things that can help you get him back."

Hazel's heart sped up. "Like what?"

"I can make you beautiful," he said. "I can make you womanly. I can make you charming and worldly. I can make you clever." His face was now inches from hers. "I can make you belong."

The air was buzzing and Hazel couldn't seem to think. He didn't understand, that wasn't what she meant.

Or was it?

At least with Jack, she had belonged somewhere. With him gone, though, she was a misshapen piece. Was there enough magic in the woods to make her belong?

She opened her mouth to speak and the man gripped her hand. She felt a shock run through her body, and then she swayed a little and the air didn't seem like it knew how to support her. She thought of the whistle in her pocket and the boy at the other end, but he was so far away. And the man smiled again and it was a very funny kind of smile, and he whispered, "I can give you whatever you want. It won't cost anything. I'll just ask one thing in return."

A voice reached out to her like a lifesaver in the water. "Rose! Rose, what are you doing? Rose!"

A dark-haired man in a blue coat rushed up to Hazel and put his hand firmly on her arm. He sounded out of the breath. "Rose, I've been looking everywhere for you!"

"I'm not—" Hazel said. But she was very sleepy now, and something was definitely wrong, and the man was shooting her such a look, such a curious look, and she couldn't seem to finish what she was saying. Anyway, Rose was a nice name. And she didn't have one of her own, not really.

But it didn't really matter what she thought, because he was shooing the black-cloaked man away as if he were a meddlesome bat, and it was a bit funny really and Hazel thought she might laugh if only she could remember how.

"Quickly," the man said, leading her away from the marketplace. "We don't have much time."

There it was: *Tick tock. Tick tock. Tick tock.*

Hazel was all fog. "Do I know you?"

"No," the man said, looking at her with friendly green eyes. "I'm Lucas."

"Who's Rose?" she asked.

"You're Rose. Rather, you just seem like a Rose. I had to call you something so he'd think you were mine."

"I do?" No one had ever said she seemed like a Rose before. "You can call me Rose if you want."

"All right. Rose it is."

"Where are we going?"

"You need an antidote. He pressed something into your skin. It lessens your judgment. He's a wizard. Did you agree to anything?"

"I don't think so. . . ." Weren't wizards good? Dumbledore's a wizard.

"He was trying to force you into a bargain. He'd give you your heart's desire, but you would be bound to him forever. And I can tell you that's not a good proposition."

"I don't understand this place." She had said this before, but it seemed to bear repeating.

"It's all right. I do. Now, come on, we should get you home."

Nothing made sense to Hazel, and she was so sleepy, like there was a weight pulling down on her brain. But the man had his arm around her now and was guiding her forward. This arm had the weight and comfort of the one belonging to her father.

"My wife is an herbalist," the man named Lucas said. "We try to have antidotes around. There are all manner of things that can happen to you in the woods."

"I would like to go to sleep now," Hazel proclaimed.

The arm tightened around her shoulder. "I know. But stay with me. You can sleep soon."

He kept talking to her as he led her through the village to a small cottage just a five-minute walk from the market square. A large, full fairy-tale moon hung in the sky now—though Hazel could have sworn it wasn't there earlier—showing a cottage that looked like something from a movie. The thatched roof nestled over the small square house like a mushroom cap. Bright yellow curtains hung in the windows. A strip of bright flowers lay in front of the house, blooming against the cold.

"It's so pretty," said Hazel.

"Wait till you see the garden," Lucas said.

Soon Hazel was inside the kitchen of the tiny cottage, slumped in a hard wood chair, while Lucas spoke in a low voice to his wife.

Lucas's wife introduced herself as Nina. Hazel blinked up at her. She looked Indian, like Hazel, and when she smiled down at Hazel it was like something familiar but forgotten. Hazel smiled back, or at least tried to. The woman turned to the stove and began throwing things in a pot, while Lucas sat down next to Hazel and forbade her from putting her head on the table.

"So, Rose," he asked, "what's a girl like you doing in the woods like this?"

He meant to keep her talking, that was clear. He was trying to take care of her. Hazel's sleepy heart panged.

"I lost my friend," she said. She kept saying this, again and again. She'd lost her friend. That's what she was doing here.

"I'm sorry," Lucas said. "I'm very sorry."

"The white witch took him."

"Oh," said Lucas. He and his wife exchanged a glance.

"I came here to rescue him. But I need to sleep first. I'm very, very tired."

"I know," he said gently. "In a little bit."

"Then I'll go in the morning."

"Go where?" Nina asked slowly. "To the white witch?"

"Yes." Yes.

"No. You shouldn't go," she said. "It's not safe."

Hazel's heart twisted. "She has my friend."

"So you're just going to go after him? Just like that?"

". . . Yes."

"Nina . . ." Lucas motioned to his wife, then eyed Hazel. "I don't know how to ask this," he said. "But your friend, are you sure he wants to be rescued?"

"Of course he does!" She was getting tired of people asking this.

"It's just . . ." he began. "The white witch only takes people who want to go." Out of the corner of her eye, Hazel saw Nina flinch.

"No," Hazel said. "Not this time." From somewhere she heard the sound of a bird singing. Her eyes traveled out the kitchen window. It was dark, and the moon hung in the sky. She could just see the edges of the garden.

"She'll promise you things," Lucas said. "These are not things the people who come here know how to turn down."

"I need to defeat her," Hazel insisted. "Do you know how?" She looked from Lucas to Nina. They did not look at her, or at each other.

"Some things you just can't fight," Nina said quietly, after a time.

"We should talk about this in the morning," Lucas said. "Ready, Nina?"

"Here you go." Nina stood in front of her, holding out a steaming cup. It struck Hazel, suddenly, looking at the pair of them, that this could have been what her before-parents looked like. She stared up at them, the man and the woman looking down at her, full of concern and care. And she wanted to ask them things big and small, but she did not have the words.

She sipped the tea—it was thick with honey. Hazel remembered the candy her father would bring home from his trips. It was hard candy on the outside but the inside was a warm burst of actual honey, like you'd stuck your spoon into the jar when no one was looking. When she was little, she'd bite into the hard candy right away to get to the honey center. But when she got older, she learned to wait and let the filling slowly work its way out.

"You poor girl," said Nina, reaching out to rub Hazel's head. "You take your time with that. You'll feel better soon."

Out of the corner of her eye, she saw Nina move back

to the stove, her hand lingering on her husband's arm for a moment as she turned. Hazel felt the gentle touch as if it had happened to her.

Hazel remembered this. Two parents at a table. The way one would touch the other casually, a hand on the shoulder, a brush against the cheek. These unconscious gestures, like their bodies were speaking to each other— *Yes, you are here and I am here.* It had been a long time since she'd seen that.

Hazel remembered her father. He had strong arms. He used to like her stories. He took her to the Renaissance Festival two summers ago. They'd sat on bleachers in the sun, roasting like mutton, watching a jousting match. *I'm going to be a knight,* Hazel had said, feeling the lance in her hands. *No,* he'd replied, *you let others do that for you. You are a princess.*

Hazel remembered Jack. They mounted their scooters and took plastic swords and jousted on the driveway. Jack had knocked Hazel off first and she'd skinned her knee on the concrete, bright red like a berry. Jack had said it was a battle wound and smeared a cherry popsicle on himself for fake blood.

And she wondered, now, if she was trying to rescue the wrong Jack, if instead of trying to find the white witch she should look for one of her old Jacks, before any of this had happened, before he lost interest in her.

"Any better?"

Hazel nodded. "I'm sorry," she said.

"You don't have to be sorry," Nina said. "We're happy to help. And you're not the first girl we've rescued from the likes of him. Girls come into these woods thinking they can make it on their own, but . . ." Her eyes traveled to the table.

"We like to keep our eyes out," said Lucas. Nina put a hand on her husband's shoulder.

"We had a girl once," she said. "We lost her."

"Oh," said Hazel. She looked up at them, searching their eyes for some sign of recognition. She wanted to ask questions, but how do you ask people things like that? *When did you lose her, how did you lose her, did you give a baby girl up for adoption, and, do you remember, what was her name?*

"We keep trying to find her, but—" Nina shook her head. "So we try to help out other girls. Keep them safe. You can stay here as long as you need."

Hazel looked back out at the garden. She could hear the sadness in their voices, feel it hanging in the air like fog.

She'd wondered about her birth parents and if they ever wished for her, if they knew what had happened to her, if they knew she was half a world away. Or was she only a missing piece to them, a hole at the center of things, an ache that had no name?

She could not think. Her mind was too soft and thick, and not suited for things like thinking anymore.

"I think I'd like to go to sleep now," she said.

"Don't you want to see the garden?" Lucas asked.

"She can see it tomorrow," Nina said. "She should sleep. It's better." She helped Hazel out of her chair, handed her her backpack, and led her out of the kitchen. The birdsong wafted out of the main room. Hazel stopped. It sounded familiar somehow.

"Is there a bird in here?"

"Let me show you," Nina said.

She led her to the front room. There was a fire in the fireplace, shelves upon shelves of books, and two side-by-side reading chairs. And across the room on a little silver perch was a mechanical bird.

Hazel took a step closer. The bird looked like it was made out of the same colors as the flowers in front, with a rich purple body, a yellow mask, and a bright red belly. It looked like a robin that had rolled around in jewel-tinged paint. Its head moved jerkily around, and it lifted its wings and then dropped them again in a steady rhythm.

"Wow," Hazel said. "Did someone make that?"

"Lucas is a bit of an inventor," Nina said.

It sang again, lifting its head to the ceiling.

"It sounds so real."

"We had a real one once, but . . ." She shook her head. "It got away. This one is much more reliable."

"It reminds me of a bird I saw," Hazel said. She didn't realize it until the words were out of her mouth, but the song reminded her of Ben's bird sister a little.

"Really?" asked Nina. "Where?"

Hazel opened her mouth, but somewhere in the fog of her mind she remembered her promise to Ben. "Oh, you know. Wisconsin."

"Oh," Nina said. "Well, this one is marvelous. You can take it apart and see how it works. And it's never going to go away."

Hazel nodded. Yes. It was pretty. But she was very tired. And the song of the bird made her sad, somehow. So Nina led her into a small back room.

"I'm afraid it's a bit of a mess," she said.

It was. It was a small workroom. There were shelves lined with small, inscrutable tools and pieces of clockwork. On the table was scattered a number of small animal figurines made of pieces of brass. They were in various states of completion. Hazel's eyes fell on a figure with the shape of a cat. The face was off, revealing innards made of gears.

A small mattress and a thick white comforter lay in the corner of the room. They called to Hazel and she answered.

Hazel put her backpack down and crawled in, and the bed embraced her. Nina lifted the white comforter over her and gave her a smile.

"What happened to your face?" she asked gently.

"Oh. There was a witch. She scratched me."

"I'm sorry. That's the sort of thing that happens here. I think I can fix it. Tomorrow."

"That would be nice," Hazel said. What a wonderful thing to be able to take away a scar, just like that. "Are you from here?"

Nina smiled. "No one here is from here, not to begin with," she said. "Are you going to be all right?"

Her eyes were full of such tenderness, as if they had all the time in the world for her.

Hazel nodded. It was strange to wander into the fairy-tale woods and come upon a place that felt so real. "Thank you."

"You're welcome. Go to sleep, Rose. We'll talk in the morning. I'm so glad you've come."

"Me, too," said Hazel.

Chapter Nineteen

ROSE

Honey coursed through Hazel's body as she slept, running through her veins and into her heart. Her dreams were thick with it. Jack was there, climbing onto the counter and taking the jar off the top shelf where his mother thought it could not be reached. Hazel liked to use a spoon but Jack just stuck his finger in, because he was a boy.

Once Hazel skinned her knee jousting on scooters, and Jack's mom cleaned it up, wincing the whole way. Hazel was young and had the taste of stolen honey in her mouth, but she still wanted to tell Mrs. Campbell that it was going to be okay.

They used to do things like jousting. And pirates. They

had the grandest adventures. Jack liked things like super-heroes and aliens and spies. Hazel liked long, elaborate quests. They were a fellowship, come together to save the world. Her father said she was a princess. He did not see that she was a brave knight. Jack did. They saved the king-dom, again and again, and let the king have all the honor. It was the knight's job, after all.

Once Hazel started to pretend that Jack had been taken by a dragon and she was going to rescue him. Jack wouldn't play. He insisted that this would never happen, he would never get taken by a dragon, and he most certainly did not need rescuing, for he was Jack, Prince of Eternity.

Hazel jolted awake in her little bed, blanket heavy on top of her, the small room just as heavy with night. Moon-light streamed through the window and she could see the odd shapes of the half-finished clockwork animals scat-tered around the room.

What if Jack didn't want her to come?

She came in thinking she would rescue him, like some sort of story, like a little kid pretending to be a brave knight. He needed saving; therefore, she would save him. This was the way it used to work. It used to always be so simple, it was just the two of them and they could make shacks into palaces. But things change.

Jack went off on the sleigh with the white witch,

without warning or word. She could come all this way, she could break him out of his snow globe, and he would scoff and roll his eyes and say, "Hazel, stop being such a baby."

Ben had said it. And Lucas, too. The white witch would not have taken him if he didn't want to go. He wanted to leave his mom and her unseeing eyes. He was the invisible boy looking for the place where no one could find him, where he did not have to feel invisible anymore.

Why would they want to stay?

Hazel always saw him, always. But it wasn't enough for him. She wasn't enough. She could be such a baby sometimes.

Maybe rescuing him was not the point at all. Maybe Hazel was supposed to come here and find this couple in their cottage who only had a sad mechanical bird to keep them company. They had a missing piece, a hole at the center, an ache with no name. Maybe Hazel was just the misshapen piece for them.

Maybe she was Rose, after all—maybe that had been her real name. Maybe she had come into the woods and slipped into the life she was supposed to have had, if no one had wanted to give her up. Maybe the woods are where people found each other. This is what happens on journeys—the things you find are not necessarily the things you had gone looking for.

Maybe she didn't belong anywhere else because she belonged here.

Hazel got up and looked out the window. The moon shone on the garden like it had been hung in the sky for that purpose alone. The garden beckoned to her. She'd slept in her clothes, and they were damp and uncomfortable. She opened her backpack and then remembered that she didn't have a change of clothes anymore. Hazel pulled the comforter up on the bed so it was nice and neat, and then grabbed her backpack, stuffed the jacket in it, and tiptoed through the dark cottage. The mechanical bird chirped at her as she passed.

She could still taste her dreams distantly in her mind. And the memory of Nina's tea lingered in her body. There was something about it. Everything around her looked sharp, almost unnaturally so, like she could see the truth of things. Like if she looked at a box she would know what was inside.

She stepped outside, and then stopped and stared. The small garden was just a slip of earth on the side of the house, but it seemed like its own universe. The sweet, sharp scent of hundreds of flowers greeted her. Even in the night their colors sang. It was a thick, lush blanket of color—luxurious purple and electric blue and sunshine yellow and cheery red. It was like a movie version of an enchanted garden, gorgeous, vivid, and too beautiful to be real. She could dive into the purple of the violets and live there.

She felt suddenly that she wanted for nothing in the world. The flowers called to her, like they had secrets to tell—*Rose, come on.* Hazel found herself lying down on the cushioned white bench that sat among them, and their fragrance reached up to welcome her.

Sleep pulled her back immediately, wrapping her in the sort of haze that presses down on you and you're not sure it will ever let you go but you're not sure that you ever want to leave. It was so peaceful there in the fog. She wanted for nothing.

And then the flowers began to whisper to her. The noise did not belong. It pulled at her brain like longing, and Hazel wanted it to go away.

They did not stop whispering. The flowers had secrets. They had names, too, though the couple in the cottage called them Daisy, Lily, Hyacinth, Violet, Dahlia, Jasmine, Poppy, and they did not remember the ones they had before. They told Hazel that she must listen.

Daisy grew up in a house with a stream in back, and behind it were some woods. She and her friends Isabelle and Amelia played in them all the time when they were little kids, even though they weren't supposed to. Daisy's mother liked to keep her eye on them, and the trees blocked her

view. And then Daisy got sick and could not play anymore. Her friends stood by her bed telling her of the things they did, but after a while they stopped coming. Daisy snuck out of the house one morning, dragging her muscles and bones with her, and crept into the woods. She came upon a wizard who lured her in with healing whispers but did not mean her well. She ran, and a kindly couple took her in.

She was a flower now. She missed her friends and the games they'd play in the woods. They were princesses once, charged with saving the kingdom from a dragon, and whoever could defeat it would be queen. Daisy used strength, Amelia wits, and Isabelle fell in love with the dragon, because that's the sort of girl she was. She rid the kingdom of the dragon, and then made it its king.

Violet had a brother who was eight years older, and he always treated her like a doll. One day, one of the neighbor boys put a snake in her shoe and taunted her for crying. The next day her brother paid him a visit and he never bothered her again. There was a war, and her brother decided to go. He was gone two years, and when he came back he was a shell.

In the woods she fell in love with a shadow who tricked her into believing he was a man. A kindly couple took her in. They'd had a girl once, but lost her.

She was a flower now. Her brother used to pretend to

be a general. He gave her stuffed animals ranks and put them through basic training. He demoted the penguin for insubordination.

Lily was in love with a boy who promised her things. He did not keep his promises, and the heartbreak sent her into tar-thick blackness. She started taking long walks and wondered what would happen if she just kept walking. She went into the woods one day, and there the blackness was real. The cold began to tug at her, it whispered promises in her ear. A kindly couple took her in. They'd had a girl once, but lost her. She meant to leave, every day she meant to leave, but they were like the parents you think you should have, and everything tasted like honey.

She was a flower now. She could think of the boy without bringing the blackness on. In the summer they would sneak out at night and meet in the park, and now the smell of the evening air always reminded her of him. He'd push her on the swing just to make her fly. The mosquitoes ate her arms and the grass tickled her legs. When he laughed, his ears turned bright red.

Poppy had lived here ever since she could remember. She was on her own, but she got by. There were wolves in the woods, and sometimes they watched her cabin. She huddled in it until they left. There was a woodsman who came by sometimes, he had kindly eyes and an ax, and that kept the wolves away.

One day she found something near her little hut. Someone had left red ballet slippers. She could not resist them; she had never had anything like them. She danced, and she remembered the mother and the father she had had, and it was like they were there, applauding her.

But she could not stop dancing. The shoes would not let her stop. She was going to dance herself to death. The woodsman found her. He said the shoes must be cursed. He said he could save her life, but she would have to lose her feet. This is the price we pay. She ran away, and Lucas and Nina rescued her and took her in. They were like the parents you think you should have, and everything tasted like honey. And then one day she took root.

She remembered her real parents, now. They'd died when she was three, but she had them again, and even though she was a flower she knew what it was like to have them shining with pride when she danced. She held on to them, and the memory of them kept her, and tended to them all.

Hazel remembered, too. She remembered her mother— not her before-mother, but the one she had always known. Hazel was in bed pretending not to cry, and her mother was stroking her forehead, whispering to her gently. She told Hazel that everything was going to be okay. She told her that she would just work twice as hard for Hazel. She told her that they were going to take care of each other. It was just the two of them now, but they had each other. It was going to be okay.

And then she told Hazel that it was time to wake up. That she needed to wake up. *Hazel, baby, you must wake up now.*

Hazel woke up. The flowers watched her with open faces. She sat up and looked at them. They seemed to expect something of her. She could feel the weight of her mother's hand on her forehead, the caress of her whisper in her ear.

Her hand flew to the backpack where the whistle was. She needed help now. And then her hand retracted. Flashes of conversation played in her head. Ben said:

This couple found us and they brought us to their cottage and they took care of us.

They were like real parents, you know?

They wanted to keep her, I guess.

There was a reason the birdsong was the same. Lucas and Nina must have moved on to flowers, to things that couldn't fly away.

Hazel could have stayed. She could have taken root. She wanted to be a Rose, somebody's Rose, their Rose—and she would have been company for the flowers. She had new memories to give them, new people to tell them of, people who would help tend to them and keep them. But they warned her. They saved her.

Hazel was nobody's Rose. For better or for worse.

You have to go, the flowers told her.

She took the canteen out of her backpack and drizzled them with the water Ben had given her the day before. It was all she had to give them.

And then a light turned on in the house behind her. Hazel dropped the canteen, slung her backpack over her shoulders, and rushed to the gate.

She was not fast enough. The back door creaked open. Hazel whirled around. Nina appeared on the step in a bathrobe.

"Rose, what are you doing?" Nina said, coming toward her. "You should be in bed."

"My name isn't Rose. It's Hazel. And I'm leaving." There, that sounded brave. Hazel took a step toward the gate.

"What? Why?" Hazel could not see Nina's face in the dark, but her voice was full of concern.

"Why?" Hazel motioned around at all the flowers. It was the only answer she could give.

"Oh." Nina came toward Hazel, her hands out. "I know. It's hard to understand. But they needed us. These girls came into the woods because they were lost. We took them in. We take care of them. We tend to them. We give them what they need."

"You turn them into flowers!" Hazel took a step back.

"That's the only way," Nina said. "It's the only way we can make sure they don't suffer anymore."

"But . . . you didn't ask them. You just kept them."

"Young people don't always know what's best. Especially the ones that come in here. They're lost. They need us." She looked at the ground and added, "It's too hard to be human."

Hazel could only shake her head.

Nina tilted her head and her voice softened. "We could keep you. We would take care of you. You wouldn't have to worry about anything anymore. This would be home."

She was looking at Hazel lovingly, pleadingly, as if it mattered to her whether or not Hazel stayed.

Hazel stared at Nina. The wizard had made her suggestible, she knew this. The honeyed tea was no antidote, she knew this, too. Still. It was possible. It was possible that this woman gave up a baby girl once, a girl with only a dream of a name, and then the grief of it drove her into this place. It was possible.

"I have to go," Hazel said, taking another step to the gate.

"To what?" Nina asked. "Back out there to the wolves? The wizards at the marketplace? To the white witch? Back

home, to whatever brought you here in the first place? Ro—
Hazel, we can keep you safe. We"—her voice softened—"*I*
can take of you."

"I have to save my friend," Hazel said, trying to keep
the words from trembling.

"But"—Nina tilted her head—"he chose something
else, don't you see? He doesn't want you anymore."

Hazel glanced at the ground, and then looked back up
at Nina. "It doesn't matter."

Nina gazed at her searchingly. "Doesn't it?"

Of course it mattered. The mattering of it filled her up
and she threatened to burst with it. But it wasn't the only
thing that mattered.

Hazel could only shrug.

"Please," Nina said, her voice almost a whisper. "Don't
go there. It's a cruel place. "

"So is this," Hazel said quietly. She half believed it.
There were worse fates than being a flower. But there were
better ones, too. And it was her puff of wool.

Nina took another step forward, and Hazel could see
her eyes now, see all the things in them. She swallowed,
turned, and pushed through the gate into the night.

She'd thought the cottage was in the middle of a small
neighborhood—that's what she'd seen when Lucas led her

from the market square. But when she went through the garden gate she found herself in a clearing in the middle of the woods. Of course. That is what Lucas and Nina needed, and the woods let them make it.

Hazel looked back at the cottage, thought of Nina standing behind the gate, eyes full of pain and longing, a longing she could fill. And then she turned and ran.

She could not get Poppy's story out of her head. Her mind flashed to the dancing girl in the marketplace. Hazel had seen that something was wrong. And if she had thought about it, she would have put the pieces together: the woodsman on the path, the sudden appearance of the red shoes. The woodsman had left the shoes for her to find. He lost his daughter, he came into the woods, he made some cursed dancing shoes. *The woods does funny things to people,* Ben had said.

But she didn't think about it. She had been too tired, too focused on herself.

It had been hours ago, or maybe days. There was nothing Hazel could do, though she felt like stripping off her own skin. She was good for nothing, and should have been left to take root.

She hated this place. Nothing made sense. Nothing worked as it was supposed to. She was supposed to be learning things as she went along, gaining strength for her final battle. All she was doing was losing things, one thing at a time.

She headed into the cold, for that would lead her to Jack. Because he needed rescuing. That was all. She'd lost her friend, and she might never get him back. But at least she could save him. Whoever he is now. Maybe he had chosen to come here, but he could not stay in this place.

She kept going. She reached a small footpath that stretched itself into the cold night. She joined it, and kept going.

Jack believed in something—he believed in white witches and sleighs pulled by wolves, and in the world the trees obscured. He believed that there were better things in the woods. He believed in palaces of ice and hearts to match. Hazel had, too. Hazel had believed in woodsmen and magic shoes and swanskins and the easy magic of a compass. She had believed that because someone needing saving they were savable. She had believed in these things, but not anymore. And this is why she had to rescue Jack, even though he might not hear what she had to tell him.

There were so many Jacks she had known, and he had known so many Hazels. And maybe she wasn't going to be able to know all the Jacks that there would be. But all the Hazels that ever would be would have Jack in them, somewhere.

The truth was, he had been getting more and more scratchy and thick lately. And maybe he'd been more and more interested in being with Tyler and the boys on the bus. And maybe he'd hung out with them at recess more and more. Because sometimes when you are scratchy and thick you don't want to be sitting in a shack with someone pretending it's a palace, especially someone who can tell you are scratchy and thick, especially someone who tries to remind you who you really are.

Maybe he didn't want to know.

The boys wouldn't come to save him. Only Hazel would. And maybe that's why the boys would win.

She felt the memory of her mother's hand again. *It's all going to be okay.* She would like to hear that now, even if it was a lie. Because some lies are beautiful. Stories do not tell you that.

And who was telling her mother it was going to be okay? What did her mom think happened to her? She'd be so worried she'd break in two. Hazel didn't even know how long she'd been gone. How long had her mother been missing Hazel for, worrying about her? Had it been so long that the panic had settled into something dull and unrelenting?

How long did it take for her to figure out Hazel wasn't coming back from Mikaela's, had never gone to Mikaela's, that there was no school project at all? She'd know Hazel had lied to her, betrayed her, that her little girl had crossed a line.

Hazel should have done something—left a note, pretended she was going to go visit Jack's aunt Bernice. Something. She was so busy thinking about the one she needed to rescue she didn't think at all about the one she was leaving behind. She was supposed to take care of her mother, too. She was not supposed to be sipping honey tea with people who are just like the parents you think you are supposed to have. Her mother was what she had.

The woods were dark, but she could still see the path, feel the cold. There was nothing for Hazel to do but keep going. But as much as she had to keep going, she had to come back, too. She had to survive this. She could not leave her mom alone.

She walked on. The trees were thinner now, less like the trees of giants. She saw signs of another village in the distance—she smelled smoke and saw the faint glow of something like civilization. But there was nothing for her there. She had to go get Jack now, and anyway, she was safer out here with the wolves.

Chapter Twenty

MATCHLIGHT

The footpath led Hazel to a bigger path, the sort that might accommodate carts. Hazel eyed the open path warily and then moved over to the side, creeping along the trees like a stalking wolf. She could stick her hand up in the air and feel where the cold was pulling her forward. Somewhere in the distance was the lair of the white witch, cold radiating out from it like heat from a fire.

She let it pull her in.

After a time, she found that there was a thin layer of frost on the ground, sparkling in the moonlight. Slowly she became conscious that she was shivering, that the cold had worked its way through her skin into her blood and bone. Her breath came out of her mouth in puffs. Her chest felt tight and her lungs ached. She stopped and shuddered. She ran her hands along her arms, and then got down her backpack and took out her jacket and her mittens and hat and put them on. She would even have worn the third-grade ones.

The green jacket did its best to warm her. It was a hard job. The cold had snuck up on her so stealthily she didn't even notice it had invaded her until was too late. Hazel breathed away the trembling and thought warm thoughts. And then she went on.

The night in the forest would not relent. It seemed like it had been hours since she'd left the cottage, that the sun should be coming up now. But she didn't know for sure— maybe she was done with the sun now, maybe night was all that the woods would give her.

Eventually she realized she was hungry, and that she had been hungry for a long time. She stopped and opened her backpack. She had two energy bars left to get her through.

She sighed and took one out. She would only eat half of it. She could make this last. Then she would eat half of the next half, and on and on. She could go for a while that way, anyway, getting slowly used to less and less food until one bite of energy bar felt like a feast.

Hazel was just about to unwrap the bar when she

noticed a flash of light up ahead. It burned for a few moments, and then died out. Then again—another flash, a slowly dimming glow, and then darkness. Then, from close by, a voice said: "Oh!"

Hazel had had enough of people. With every one she met, the woods became worse. She tucked the bar back in her backpack and started to sneak in the opposite direction.

She did not walk for long, for an enormous white wolf appeared a few paces in front of her. It sat on its haunches and stared at her, in the way the wolves did, its perfect coat glimmering in the moonlight. And though her heart sped up and her stomach clenched, Hazel found herself staring back at the wolf. She was done running from them. Hazel and the wolf eyed each other as the wind danced around them. And then the wolf got up and walked several paces to the right, and then turned its head toward her and fixed its gaze on her again.

"What?" Hazel said.

It went back to the place it had started from, and then did the same thing again.

"You want me to follow you?" Hazel said.

The wolf gazed at her, walked a few paces back, and then forward again. It looked at her. And she stepped forward.

In woods where the woodsmen told lies, maybe it was the wolves who told the truth.

The wolf turned and walked back the way Hazel had come. Hazel followed behind, trying to move as stealthily as the creature. Up ahead there was another flash of light, just as before. The wolf moved a few steps toward it, then stopped. It looked at Hazel, and then looked ahead.

"You want me to go there?"

The wolf gazed at her another moment, then disappeared into the night.

Hazel crept on ahead. She had decided to throw her lot in with the wolves, and there was no going back now. She followed the dimming light into a clearing and back onto the path.

There was a girl a few years older than Hazel sitting on a tree stump next to the big path. She did not belong out here on this cold night. All she wore was a patched-up thin brown dress, a little shawl wrapped around her shoulders, and slippers. She was visibly shivering.

The girl did not notice her. She had in her hands a lit match and was staring into the flame as if it held wonders.

She must be bewitched, Hazel thought. Someone had caused her to be so confused she'd wandered half-naked into the middle of the woods. She was hypnotized by the light and didn't know the danger she was in. Someone had done this to her, and Hazel was not going to leave this one behind. The wolves would not let her.

She approached the girl carefully. "Are you all right?" she asked, trying to keep her voice steady.

The girl looked up at Hazel with dull eyes. She had dead-looking blond hair and a too-thin shadowy face. Her skin had been blanched by the night's cold, and her cheeks looked blue-black. Her body trembled against the air as if the sky scared her. She looked like a blotchy, fading ghost.

"Hey," Hazel said, keeping her voice soft. "Are you okay? Did someone do something to you?"

The girl blinked at Hazel. "I'm fine," she said. "Where am I?"

"You're . . . you're in the woods. How did you get out here?"

"Oh," said the girl, her voice thin and vague. "I live back near the village."

She nodded to a place somewhere beyond them.

"Come on, we have to get you home."

"I can't," said the girl, her eyes on the fading match. "I can't go home until I've sold all the matches." She nodded to a bunch of long matches in her dress pocket. "I was selling all night, but— Oh!"

The match in her hand had gone out. She dropped it, and in one motion grabbed another one from her dress and struck it against a small tinderbox. A flame burst from it into the night, and the girl stared into it and exhaled.

Hazel grabbed her arm. It was shaking. "It's freezing. I'm sure they didn't mean—"

"Oh, he meant it," the girl said, still staring into the flame, and in the match light Hazel noticed that her arm was covered in bruises.

No one is from here, Nina had said. Once upon a time this girl lived in the real world, and she came into the woods looking for something. And what she found was this.

"I'll buy them!" Hazel said. "How much do you need?" She began to shrug off her backpack.

"Fifty kroner," the girl said.

"Oh."

"It's all right," said the girl. "The matches are magic."

"They are?" Hazel asked warily.

"Yes. I never knew. But look!" She stared back into the flame.

Hazel followed her eyes. She saw nothing but dancing fire against a blue girl. "What are you looking at?"

"That's my grandmother," the girl said, voice hushed, eyes glued to the flame. "She's made dinner. She makes the most wonderful turkey, do you smell it?" The girl was staring into the fading flame as if inside it was the secret truth of the world. But they were ordinary matches, and her visions were the deluded comfort of a dying mind.

Hazel could feel her heart lose its solidity and diffuse

slowly in her chest. She had a strong urge to grab a chunk of her own hair and pull it as hard she could. "Don't you see it?" asked the girl, voice suddenly wavering.

Hazel wanted to tell her no, to tell her to stop wondering at phantoms, because she was freezing to death and maybe starving, and they needed to find someone who could help her. But . . .

"Yes," she whispered. "I see it. It's beautiful. Where does your grandmother live?"

"Up there." The girl pointed to the sky.

"Oh," Hazel said again.

She looked at the girl and the matches. They had been real, useful things once.

And then Hazel knew what she had to do.

"Stay still," she whispered.

She removed her green jacket, then gently took the smoking match out of the girl's hand. She dressed the girl in the jacket, one arm at a time, and zipped it up. She pulled off her hat and mittens, then placed the hat on the girl's head and the mittens on her hands.

The girl hugged the jacket around herself. Her eyes widened and she stared at Hazel.

"It's warm, right?" Hazel said, trying to control her voice. "It's a nice jacket."

The girl nodded slowly. "Aren't you cold?" she whispered.

Yes. "No," she said. "I don't have much farther to go."

"Why are you doing this?" The girl looked so bewildered, like kindness was unfathomable to her, and that broke Hazel's heart more than anything.

"Here," Hazel said, handing her one of the energy bars. "I have one more. You need to eat it."

The air had no trouble working its way through Hazel's shirt, and she felt the bite of cold on her bare hands. She blinked it away.

"There's one more thing."

Hazel reached over to the jacket and put her hand on the zipped-up pocket, feeling the familiar outline of the whistle. She unzipped the pocket and gave the whistle an almost invisible caress with her thumb. Then she blew into it three times, just as she learned to at school, and presented it to the girl.

"Blow on this," she said. "Three times, every few minutes. A boy will come. His name is Ben, and he'll help you. You tell him what happened. You tell him I gave you this. He'll take care of you. You can trust him."

Those were all the real things Hazel had left, other than the baseball which was just a fantasy, really

The girl blinked at her, and then thrust the bunch of matches into her hand. "Take these," she said. "It's the only payment I have."

"No, you have to sell them."

"Please," she said. "Take them. Please take them."

"Okay," Hazel said, if only to quiet her. "Okay."

The girl handed her the matches and the tinderbox. The wind stirred, and Hazel felt the cold tugging at her, trying to pull her to it. She belonged to it now.

Hazel opened her mouth to find some way to say good-bye, when the girl's hand flew to the apron pockets that hung down below Hazel's jacket. "I have something else!" she said.

"I don't—"

"Take it," she said, pulling a shiny something out of her pocket. "It shows you things, like the matches. But this shows you the truth. It shows you the way things really are." It was a shard of mirror, about the size of Hazel's hand. Hazel just nodded and put it in her backpack.

"Thank you," the girl said, voice soft. Her eyes had lost their vagueness now and looked at Hazel with piercing clarity. Hazel could only nod again and then turn away into the cold.

As Hazel walked on through the night, the feeling of the air biting into her took all her attention. At least it kept her from thinking about the match girl. And if she thought too hard about her, Hazel would just stop right there in the woods and wait for herself to take root. This is what it is to live in the world. You have to give yourself over to the cold, at least a little bit.

From somewhere off in the distance came the sound of Hazel's whistle blowing—once, twice, three times. Somewhere Ben, the one person in the woods who would come when she needed someone, heard the call and was coming. But not for her. Hazel was on her own.

She had nothing left, except a baseball, matches, and a broken piece of mirror. She had taken the girl's fantasy from her. She would at least keep it well.

She walked on. Her eyes were watering, her skin was chafing, her body was shivering. The ticking of the clock seemed to taunt her, as if it was marking out the time she had left. She remembered running out of the house the morning the snow fell. It had been just over a week ago, but for Hazel it felt like an epoch away. Going outside in socks and her pajamas was a game, a lark. The frozen white world offered only possibility.

The cold laughed at her now.

After a while she realized she was walking in a layer of snow. She had not noticed when it had taken over the ground. And yet it was there, all around her, like the world had transformed itself in a breath.

The snow had started to fall, too, in soft flakes that

tumbled exuberantly in the wind. They fell against Hazel's shirt, brushed against her face, a flirtation.

The wind roused itself, pushing against her softly, a whispered threat. The ground beneath her had begun to tilt, and Hazel found herself heading up an incline. Her legs whimpered at her, for that was all they could muster now. Her lungs sucked in biting air with each breath, and it invaded her body eagerly, ready to freeze her from the inside out.

Everything in her wanted to curl up under a tree—just to rest a little. If she lay down she might fall asleep and dream of warm things. She knew she should not, that her shivery mind was whispering false promises to her, that if she slept she might not wake up. And she knew that if she kept going much longer, she would no longer care.

It had been so hot last summer. The two of them lay on the sidewalk like salamanders in the sun. Hazel wondered what it would be like to melt, if you would feel yourself slowly liquefy, or if your conscious thoughts would evaporate away before you did. Jack went into his garage and pulled out an old plastic baby pool that looked like a frog and dragged it into the backyard. Then he disappeared into the house and came out with a bowl filled with ice and dumped it into the pool. "Come on," he told Hazel, prodding her with his foot like she was an overturned turtle.

They took bowls from the kitchen and filled them with as much ice as the refrigerator could give, until it sputtered and whined and groaned. They milked Hazel's refrigerator for all it was worth, then went door to door collecting from their neighbors, dumping their spoils into the plastic pool. The neighbors were parsimonious with their ice; it was going to take days to fill the pool. So Hazel flung herself into the thin layer of icy slushy watery mess and rolled around in it, numbing her skin until she was part ice cube herself.

"Get out!" Jack yelled.

"I can't! I'll melt!" Hazel yelled back. You had to be very careful when you were part ice cube.

"It's my turn!" said Jack.

"Have you no pity, sir?"

"Make way!" Jack bellowed, and then jumped into the pool. Hazel had just enough time to roll over to the side so she didn't get landed on. Jack wriggled around in the ice water like a baby otter, trying to cover as much of his body as possible.

"I'm frozen in carbonite!" Jack yelled, contorting his arms outward. The left one jabbed Hazel in the face.

Hazel took a handful of dripping ice and flung it at Jack, and Jack took his own handful and rubbed it into Hazel's hair. Soon every bit of Hazel was numb, and she and Jack lay next to each other in the pool, all the ice of the neighborhood melting in puddles around them. But Jack and Hazel were not melting. They had defeated the sun.

A gust of icy wind hit Hazel's face like a slap. The memory left. She stopped and looked around, as if she might see it scampering away. But there was nothing, of course, nothing but the black trees and the snow that worked its worm-tongued way into her sneakers. She reached in her mind for the taste of the sun, but it was gone.

The hill was only growing steeper. Still, she pressed forward. One foot, then the other. Up, and up.

And then she stopped. She had come to a plateau, and the sight before her froze her as still as a winter night.

She was staring into an endless wall of whirling, whipping, roiling snow. The wall spread over the entire horizon, and down as far as she could see. It was impossible to tell where the sky ended and the ground began, if it began at all. If she fell off the precipice she might tumble through the snow for all eternity.

The snow made it look like the very air was churning and gave a sickly cast to the night darkness. It was like she had reached the end of the world, and beyond it was this fierce emptiness that curled its way around everything like a snake, just waiting for its moment to squeeze.

A sick-hued darkness overtook Hazel. There was

ground, somewhere, and somewhere beyond that there was a palace, and somewhere beyond that was a witch, and somewhere beyond her was a boy who did not want her to come, and she would not come, could not come, because she could not defeat the winter. She was going to collapse here. She would fail.

And then the cold began to whisper to her. *Come,* it said. *This is nothing. You can survive this. Come, I will help you. Come, you belong here. Come, I will show you.*

She took a step forward, whether of her own will or because the cold was dragging her now she did not know.

That's right. This is nothing. Come.

There should have been the sound of the wind, there should have been her breath and beating heart, but she could hear absolutely nothing but the whispering of the winter.

This is nothing. And you are nothing.

She took another step, and stumbled. The ground was plummeting downward now.

You are nothing.

There was a starving girl. You gave her things and then left her like a beggar on the street, and for what?

There was a couple in the cottage. You could have given them something, but you left. And for what?

There was a dancing girl in the marketplace. You could

have helped her, but you left. And for what?

There was a boy and his bird sister. He helped you, and you gave him nothing.

There was a swanskin, and you thought it might make you beautiful.

There were red shoes, and you thought they might make you graceful.

There was a threshold and a magical woods, and you thought they might make you a hero.

There was a boy, and he was your best friend.

Your father left you. You left your mother.

Come, the wind said, *and I will blow you away.*

Come, the snow said, *and I will bury you.*

Come, the cold said, *and I will embrace you.*

Come. Come.

And so she did.

Chapter Twenty-one

JACK,
PRINCE OF ETERNITY

There once was a boy named Jack who lived with the ice and snow. His home was a small ice floe in the middle of an inky lake.

There was a woman who visited him sometimes. She called herself a witch. She said she could be like a mother to him, and that sounded like something good. But when she came he knew there was a great hole at the center of himself. He could never find the right words for her, even though she smiled and patted him on the head and told him he was good.

Sometimes she gave him a kiss on his forehead, and that, too, seemed like something good.

The kisses kept the dreams at bay. Those dreams flitted

through his consciousness like the taste of a forgotten food. There was an invisible boy in them, he remembered that much, and Jack felt bad for the boy. He did not like these dreams—even the memory made him feel like he was melting. He did not understand why he couldn't dream of ice, where he belonged.

The witch came and asked him questions and pronounced him delightful, but he could see no delight in her eyes. Amusement, perhaps. Maybe even mirth. But never delight. He was failing her, and if he failed she would send him to the too-warm dream world. He would melt away.

She brought him things sometimes. She brought him a car made of wood, some playing cards, a schoolbook with math problems in it. He didn't need those things, but he didn't want to disappoint her. He pretended to enjoy them, but she saw right through him, as clearly as if she were looking through ice.

"We'll find something you like," she said.

And he wanted to explain that he wanted nothing but her approval, but he was afraid. So he only nodded and thanked her, and she smiled, and the smile made him feel starved.

"You are such a delight!" she said.

He was not. There was a hole at his center, and she could see right into it.

And then one day she brought him something new. She appeared on his ice floe like the sun.

"It's a puzzle," she said, unfolding her hands. "Do you like puzzles?"

He did. He knew he did. Puzzles fit together. He smiled up at her.

She bent down and placed a pile of small ice shards in front of him. "Good. These are the puzzle pieces. You can spell words with them. If you spell the right one, I will give you your heart's desire."

He picked up a shard and looked it. It felt good in his hands. Right. He held it up, and a sunbeam shone through it as if it was reaching for him.

"What is the right word?" he asked. He could not take back the words once they came out. He was such a small, shriveled-up thing.

She smiled and brushed his cheek with her ice hands. "You have to figure that out on your own."

Eternity. The word popped into his head. Maybe the sun had taken pity on him.

"Aren't you a delight?" she said. He looked down at the puzzle shards. They were made of odd, jagged angles. He reached a finger out to touch one of the points. He felt nothing, but a small dome of red blood rose out of his finger pad. He eyed it curiously, then put his hands on the shards and began to move them around the ice. He let out a breath he did not know he was holding. Manipulating the ice shards felt like coming home. His heart stirred, and he looked up at the witch.

"You like that?" she said.

He nodded, a smile on his face.

"You are fascinating," she said, cold eyes sparkling.

And he knew that she meant it, and he despaired, for he might never feel this way again. "Do you want me to solve it?" he asked, nodding toward the puzzle.

"Of course," she said. "I want you to be happy."

Then he would solve it. He put his head down and lost himself to the ice.

Chapter Twenty-two

THE SNOW QUEEN

Hazel could not see a path ahead of her, but still she moved forward into the great seething nothing—for she had put her faith in the cold now, as it was all she had left. The nothing greeted her hungrily—swirling around her, pulling at her, whipping at her skin. It would soon devour her. Or it already had.

Hazel hunched over and threw her hands in front of her face, as if there was any protection to be had. The air crackled and pushed her forward as her feet tried to make sense of the ground. They couldn't, and she slipped, and then tumbled down the hill like a flake in the wind. Hazel skidded and rolled, the snow clinging to her, until the incline eased and released her. She lay in the snow, a pile of bones, feeling the air whip around her. She could stay like this. She could stay like this.

But she didn't. The cold pulled her forward, still, and so she picked herself up.

She thrust her arms above her head again and then eased herself down the hill, one slippery step at a time. Her clothes were covered in snow, but it didn't seem to matter as she was mostly snow herself now. She breathed it, in and out. It collected in her gasping lungs. The snow was colonizing her, breath by breath.

She reached flat land and picked her way forward, through snow that rose and fell like frozen waves. The wind did not let the snow settle on the ground for long—it blew it up to the sky as fast as the sky could pour it down, and all Hazel could do was push through.

She could not see more than a few feet in front of her, so she did not look. She knew what was out there because it was all a part of her now—the endless churning darkness, the shadowy snowdrifts that collected in the wind and blew apart again.

She huddled her shoulders together, as if trying to make herself as inconsequential as possible, and still trudged forward. One step. Another. Another.

It should have been determination pulling her forward, the surety of her quest, the nobility of her heart. It should have been love, it should have been faith, or at least hope. But she had nothing like that inside of her. She had nothing inside her at all.

And still she went forward.

Somewhere ahead there was a boy who had been her best friend. She had known so many versions of him, she carried all of them with her. Here, he waggled his eyebrows through a classroom window; here, he sent her best super-hero pitch sailing through the sky; here, they sat in the shrieking shack oblivious to the world's crushed-up beer cans; here, he appeared wearing an eye patch and six-year-old Hazel felt the pieces click into place.

But snowdrifts and night were overtaking her, and Hazel only had room for so much. The Jacks left her, one at a time. The wind embraced them eagerly.

The snowflakes had turned to ice, and the pellets whipped against her face. The wind seemed like it might tear off her skin. The snow was nearly at her waist, and still she could see nothing ahead. One step. Another. It was not survivable, the cold and the tumult and the endless sickening sky. So she hardened her skin against the wind, her blood against the cold, her heart against the despairing sky

I feel nothing, she whispered, as the ice hit her skin, as the wind beat against her, as the snow menaced around her. *I feel nothing. I feel nothing.*

She was as pointless and gray as the world.

And she moved on—muscle, bone, and blankness.

And then. There. A breath. The wind released her. The snow settled itself. The cold eased. Hazel stumbled forward, and then stopped.

She could feel nothing at first but stillness. Her body did not know what to do with it. The *tick tock* of the clock was gone, and Hazel missed it like her own heartbeat.

Hazel shuddered as the wind danced around her gently, as if this was all there had ever been between them. She wiped the snow from her eyes, and it fell agreeably away. And she looked up.

She was standing in the middle of a vast plain in the snow-shimmer night. All around her was still. There was an eternity of sky above her. There was no sign of anything else—the woods, the hills, the storm. The horizon stretched on around her.

But she was not alone. There was a palace just ahead, sitting in the middle of the plain like a gift. It was simple— a small square with a dome framed by four minarets. It looked like it had been sculpted out of snow.

Hazel stared at the palace. It was not the same. It was longer and a little more elegant and more feminine. But it reminded her of the fortress in Jack's sketchbook, of the place where no one could ever find him. It was like

this plain had birthed it, just for Jack, and now it presided proudly over this kingdom of nothing.

The glimmering palace tugged at her, and Hazel gave herself to it, even though she was nothing. She was a lamentable splotch, her black hair and brown skin and green shirt and blue jeans and purple backpack a speck in this eternal whiteness.

Inside the palace was the white witch. Hazel was supposed to defeat her, though she could not even manage fifth grade. Still. She dragged her shivering, breaking body the last few steps to the palace, because she had come all this way, and now she was here.

What are you going to do now, you cold splotch? Knock?

What else was there to do?

Hanging in the middle of the front door was a solid ring of ice. Hazel reached up and grabbed it. It did not feel cold to her bare hands, and whether that was because it was really glass or because she was so frozen that ice felt like wood to her, she did not know.

Hazel banged the knocker down. The sound echoed through the white valley.

Silence. One heaving breath. Two. Three. Then the door opened.

Hazel did not know what she'd expected. Servants. Minions. Something. But she did not expect the door to be opened by a tall, shimmering woman in white, with eyes of ice and skin like snow and a dress that looked like it would evaporate in the sunlight. A rush of cold slammed into Hazel, and of dread, and of awe—so much that she took a step backward. Her feet twitched again, like they might want to flee, if only they could remember how, if only she were ever going to be able to move again.

People feared snowstorms once. Hazel read about this all the time. Pioneers opened their front doors and saw they'd been entombed in snow overnight. They walked across malevolent swirling whiteness and did not know if they would survive. Nature can destroy us in a blink. We live on only at its pleasure.

That was what looking at the witch was like.

The witch tilted her white head, as if Hazel were a great curiosity. "You made it," she said.

Hazel shivered and clattered as the witch appraised her. She was desperate for warmth, but could only search for it in the witch's eyes. There was none to be had. Still, she kept looking.

"You poor dear," said the witch, with a voice like bells. "Let's warm you up. Come inside."

And there was nothing to do but follow.

The witch led Hazel through an empty white front hall. Her movements were like floating. She did not seem real, or possible. She was as substantial as the snow. And yet the very air seemed to bow to her.

Hazel found herself in a parlor-like room. The walls were light blue, like the color Hazel had picked for her own living room, only these walls were made out of some kind of light. Translucent curtains hung in front of two windows, protecting the room from the night outside. There was a long white chaise longue and two tall, curvy white arm-chairs. Between them sat a small table on which perched a crystal statue of a ballerina.

The witch motioned to one of the chairs in a long, graceful gesture that made Adelaide's swan arms look jerky and pained in comparison.

Hazel fell against the chair. It embraced her.

"Take this," said the witch, picking up a large white fur. She wrapped it around Hazel's shoulders, and Hazel sank into it. She would have taken anything from her.

"Is that better?" the witch asked.

It was. Hazel was tucked into the furs like a baby cub. She could stay that way forever.

The witch settled herself into the chaise. "I'm sorry about the difficulty of your journey. This winter has been particularly harsh."

Hazel huddled in the furs, trying to take in the witch in front of her. It was just like being out freezing in the woods, how all you wanted in the universe was to curl up under a tree and fall asleep. And you knew it meant death. But it didn't matter.

"It wasn't so bad," Hazel found herself saying.

"Good," said the witch. "It is a difficult journey, and you are such a small girl."

Hazel winced. *Splotch.*

"So," the witch said, leaning in, "what brings a girl like you to me?"

"I lost my friend," Hazel said. As she spoke the words, she felt the snow-touched darkness seep back into her.

"I'm sorry," said the witch. "It can be quite cruel out there. The world is no place for young girls."

"He left me," Hazel said.

"I know. I'm glad you've come." Hazel searched the witch's eyes for some sign that the words were true. But there was nothing but cold curiosity. Of course not—what about her would gladden a witch?

Hazel looked away. Her eyes fell on the crystal ballerina statue. Its arms were up and its feet were in perfect third position. Hazel's feet twitched.

Then she blinked and straightened and shrugged the furs off. What was she doing? "No, wait. You took him. I came to take him back."

"Oh!" said the witch, her head slowly tilting to the

side. "I see! That's very interesting. No one's ever done that before."

"I came to take him back," Hazel repeated. "Where is he?" Her voice was shaking. That was the point where she was supposed to sound tough, like she was someone to be reckoned with, like she was the sort of person witches should listen to. Was this really her plan? She sounded like a child.

"Why," said the witch, "he's right out there." She extended an arm toward the window behind her.

"What?" Hazel looked from the witch to the window, then pushed herself off the chair.

She hurried to the window and opened the curtain. In back of the palace was a giant lake. Patches of ice floated gently on top of dark water. And in the distance Hazel could see a small, dark form crouched on one of them, perfectly framed by the window, like a piece of three-dimensional art. He was moving, she could see that much. But that's all she could tell.

Jack.

"You see?" said the witch, her voice in Hazel's ear.

Hazel whirled around. The witch was standing right next to her.

"What's he doing there? Is he okay?"

"He's safe," said the witch. "You don't have to worry."

"But . . . he'll freeze out there."

The witch's brow furrowed. "But he's already frozen." She said this as if it should be comforting.

"He's . . . what?"

"Well, it's just his heart that's frozen, really."

Hazel stared up at the witch.

"Something landed in his eye," the witch said, clasping her hands together. "Something . . . harmful. It went to his heart, you see. And so I froze it. It was for his own good."

"I don't understand."

"You are a very small girl," said the witch.

Hazel opened her mouth but had nothing to say. She could see Jack out of the corner of her eye. He seemed to be moving something around with one hand. He was totally focused on whatever was in front of him, like he was when he was drawing. And suddenly all her Jacks came rushing back. "I want him back now. He's my friend. I miss him and I want him back." Hazel's voice cracked. How she hated the weakness of her human heart.

"I see," said the witch. She turned her full gaze on Hazel. "You feel quite empty without him, don't you?"

The eyes pried at her, and Hazel could only nod.

The witch leaned in, her voice soft. "He was the thing that made you belong, after all. He made all the pieces fit together. And without him . . ." The witch moved her hands in the air.

Hazel's gaze snapped to the floor, lest she see herself in the witch's eyes.

"It's funny. You came through the woods for him, and he never even mentioned you."

Hazel's heart twisted. She would give anything not to feel this way.

"I don't think you know how to get by without him, do you? That's why you came. You can't survive out there." She motioned vaguely out the window. Whether she meant in the storm or in the real world, Hazel did not know, but it didn't matter. The witch rested a long finger on her cheek and shook her head. "You could stay," she said. "You could be with him forever. It would be better for you."

Hazel could not resist, she looked up at the witch's eyes and searched them, desperately. She could search them forever if she thought one day there might be something there for her.

But there wasn't and there never would be.

"No," Hazel said. "I have to go home, and I have to take Jack with me."

"Ah," said the witch. "You are a very small girl." She turned her eyes from Hazel, and Hazel wanted to go out and give herself to the storm.

"If you wish to live your life out there, that is your

choice," the witch continued. "But as for your friend, you do not know what's best. Look at him." She motioned out the window. "He wants for nothing. Would you really take that from him?"

"Yes," Hazel said.

"You know you'll never get him back," she said. "Not really. Even if you take him, it won't be the same."

Hazel looked at the ground. "It doesn't matter," she said in a whisper. That's not what this was about. Not anymore. "What do you want?"

The witch raised one careful eyebrow. "I? I want nothing," she told Hazel. "Don't you see? I want nothing." She waved her hand in the air. "Your Jack came to me of his own free will. If he chooses to leave, I will not stop him."

"If I can get him to leave, you'll let us go," Hazel said.

The witch opened up her arms to the air. "Certainly. But I don't think he'll choose to leave. He gave his heart very freely."

Hazel felt her stomach rise up into her throat. The witch was standing over her, looking so pleased with herself, looking as if Hazel should be pleased, too, and Hazel could barely breathe for all the coldness coming from her.

"Remember," she said, fixing her eyes on Hazel. "I'm always here."

Hazel let herself live for a moment in the witch's

unwanting eyes, and then broke away. "I'm going," she said, and walked toward the door.

"Hazel," said the witch. Hazel turned around. The witch was standing perfectly erect. She seemed to loom in the room, and her eyes were like a storm.

"Know this," she said, her voice as clear as a shard of glass. "If you take him away, he will change. And someday he will be a man, and you will not even know him, and he will only think of you with a passing smile."

At least he would think of me, Hazel wanted to say.

And she turned. Something released inside of her, some cold inexorable pulling.

It was not supposed to be this easy. This was to be the final confrontation. There was to be struggle, torment, despair. But the witch—who was the only person in the woods who wanted nothing—was not what Hazel had to defeat.

And so Hazel left. She walked through the palace and outside, back into the terrible cold. And then she was afraid. For this was her battle now. She took a deep breath and took a step into the snowbanks, and another, and began to fight her way to Jack.

Chapter Twenty-three

ᴘUZZLES

J ack could not make the pieces fit. He worked dili-
gently, constantly, but every time he made something
fit together, another problem presented itself. The pieces
made him promises, but the promises were lies. The shards
had secrets. He was never going to finish.

He was afraid she would stop coming, that he would
disappoint her—or even worse, bore her. She would lose
interest, not even notice him anymore. He would not give
up, though. She would not like that.

And she had not come since giving him the puzzle. So
when he sensed someone coming from the palace toward
him, his head snapped up.

He saw a small, dark shape struggling its way through

the snow toward the lake. It was not the witch.

He felt like he'd been plunged into the dark water. She was not coming.

His hands moved back to the puzzle, but after a few moments his eyes flickered back to the shape. It was a girl, and she was made of colors.

She was standing at the edge of the lake now. She seemed very small. Something about the girl tugged at him, and he wished the witch were there to kiss him on the forehead and make it go away.

He looked down, and one of the pieces called to him. Its edges clarified before his eyes and he understood it. Or thought he did. He took one of the small sections he'd been able to make and tried to add the piece to it, but it would not fit.

His eyes flickered upward again. The girl was still there. She was edging her way onto the lake now. She picked up one foot and set it carefully onto the ice, and then the other. She slipped a little, and her arms shot out to the sides.

Jack had never seen anyone approach him on the lake before. The witch always just appeared. The ice seemed a treacherous thing to walk on. And the girl was having trouble. She moved as lightly as a baby bird, but still she bobbled and slid.

The ice floated on the dark water in broken pieces—

large versions of the puzzle Jack had at his feet. The girl took big, careful steps over the cracks in the ice, moving in wobbly slow motion. And then she came upon a crack too big to step over. She stared at the dark water, and at the patch of ice just out of reach. She hugged herself again, and her eyes traveled ahead and met his. She looked at him so sadly. He wished he could help, but he could not make the pieces fit together.

The girl's face tightened, and she took a couple of uneasy steps away from the edge of the ice floe, squeezed her arms to her sides, and leapt over the dark crevice. She landed at the edge of the next floe and slipped. Her feet flew up from under her, and she contorted herself in the air so she would not fall backward. The side of her face thwacked onto the ice, water splashed up at her hair and her feet. She pushed herself up, grimacing and holding her head. Jack looked down at his puzzle.

Even the pieces he had fit together seemed wrong now. Everything he did seemed to make it worse.

He moved one of the pieces around, thinking its secrets might reveal themselves that way. He was surprised to look up and see the girl standing in front of him, looking down at him like he held her life in his hands instead of shards of ice. She was big-eyed and shivering, with wet shoes and hair. Her face was dark where she had hit the ice. Her chest heaved up and down. She had an enormous scar on her cheek.

He put the piece he was holding down and looked up at her. Her eyes were darker than the lake. And they welled as they looked at him, as if he was the one who had almost fallen through the ice.

He was not worth her tears.

He missed the witch.

He was nothing.

Chapter Twenty-four

OBJECT MEMORY

Hazel stared at the frozen remnant of her friend. His skin was tinged with blue, his eyelashes and hair were covered in frost. He was hard and dull, and there was no life to him at all.

She could feel that her head was shaking and her eyes had tears in them. She had to work to take in a breath, because her body would not breathe in a world where Jack could look like this.

She leaned down and put her hand on his shoulder. "Jack," she whispered.

He flinched. "You're warm," he said.

She drew back.

"Jack," she said again, because that was his name, and

that, at least, was something she could give him. "It's Hazel. Jack, we have to go home!"

Surely there was something better to say than this. But she could not think of anything else in the whole world.

He tilted his head at her, like her words made no sense to him. Like he was already home.

"No," she said, shaking her head quickly. "No, listen. . . ." Hazel closed her eyes. All this way, and she had nothing. "Jack. You're Jack. . . . Please. Here, look." She took down her backpack and got out the broken shard of mirror the match girl had given her.

"You're Jack," she said, putting the mirror in front of him. "Jack Campbell. Do you see?" And you are made of baseball and superheroes and castles, and of lots of Hazels-past, even if you lost them to the wind, it doesn't matter.

Jack looked into the shard of mirror, and his eyes widened in surprise. As he stared, his face darkened. Hazel glanced down and then started. The image in the mirror was Jack, but ten times worse—dark blue and seemingly made out of cracked ice. She let out a gasp.

Jack looked up at her, eyes wide. "He's terrible."

"No, no," she said, drawing the mirror back. "He's not. You're not. Jack . . ."

Jack blinked at her. His eyes fell warily to the mirror shard again as if it might confirm a terrible truth, and

Hazel tossed it aside.

"Um, I'm sorry," she said, struggling valiantly to keep her voice steady. "Forget that. That's nothing." She needed to warm him up, that was it. She reached into the backpack again and pulled out the matches and the tinderbox. She tried to strike the match, but her hands were shaking so badly she couldn't. A tear spilled out of her eye, and she rubbed it away quickly.

She tried again, and with a *psst* the match was lit. She held it close to him and whispered, "Do you feel that? It's warm." The last part sounded like a plea.

He looked at her, confused. Hazel's heart buried itself in her chest. What was she thinking? Like one match had any power against all this cold.

His eyes went to the flame. And then something passed over his face, and he peered at the flame like it had a secret to tell him.

"What is it?" Hazel asked, trying to control her voice. "Do you see something?"

He shook his head, but kept staring.

Hazel looked into the light, searching desperately for magic, because she needed it now. It was nothing but flame.

Hazel closed her eyes for a moment, and then opened them again.

"I see something," she said, her words a whisper.

He looked up at her.

"I do," she said, trying to sound more sure. "I see you at your house. Do you remember your house? You live next door to me. Your kitchen is bigger than mine, and yellow-er, and it's got these big blotchy flowers that you think look like soup stains, and you've got a plastic table in it." Hazel took a breath. He was still staring into the flame. "You're in the kitchen, and I'm with you. We're . . . we're sitting there in your sparkly plastic chairs making little clay guys. First you did a knight and I did a robot. I thought the robot would win. But you said that that was the obvious choice, people always pick the robots, and the knight's ability to think freely would eventually win out. Now . . . now, you're making a dragon, and I'm making a velociraptor. I'm having trouble with the neck. It's too wobbly. You tell me a T. rex would be better, and I say you always think a T. rex would be better, and then you remind me what your knight did to my robot."

The flame was dying now. But Jack still stared.

"I say," she said, her voice firm and clear, "that if you're fighting a fire-breathing dragon—and when you meet a dragon, it's best to assume it's fire breathing—what you want is speed. And the element of surprise. The dragon's going to fight hard against the T. rex, but the velociraptor won't seem like much of a threat. It's small. The dragon doesn't know it's got a sickle claw. He just sees the feathers and thinks it's a goofy dino-bird . . ."

And the flame was gone. All there was was smoke, dissolving into the lightening sky. Hazel lost her words. Her eyes went to Jack. Something had changed. He was shuddering violently now, and he dropped the shard he was holding.

"I'm cold," he said.

"Oh," she choked. "Okay. Okay. Jack . . ." She felt like someone was scooping out her chest. "Jack, I'm so sorry, I gave everything away. I don't have anything else. I—" His teeth were chattering loudly. Hazel thought she might freeze just looking at him.

"Okay, listen," she said. "I—" The backpack. Hazel took the last thing out—the baseball—and set it on the ice, and then struck another match and put it to the backpack.

The flame took hold of the backpack for a moment, then smoked and smoldered and died out.

Hazel whimpered.

"You lit your backpack on fire," Jack said.

Hazel let out a small gasp and shook her head. She was going to fail. All this way only to learn that there was nothing she could do.

Jack looked at her, shuddering and clattering and wide-eyed. His eyes fell on the baseball next to her. "What is that?" he asked.

She picked up the baseball. It was firm and real in her hands. "This?"

"Can I see that?" he asked through clattering teeth.

"Of course," she said, handing it to him.

He turned it over in his hands, considering it. His eyes fell on the big black scuff, then the signature. He studied it a moment. He moved his fingers around the soft leather, then ran his thumb slowly across the bumpy stitches.

"You gave that to me," Hazel said in a whisper. "It's a baseball, signed by Joe Mauer. He's your favorite baseball player," she added. He looked up at her, his hand firm around the baseball.

"You're going to be a catcher, someday, like him," she said. "You're going to hit nine hundred home runs, which is better than Wolverine, I think. You got the ball yourself. You went to a game with your dad last summer. The Twins won in the eleventh inning. It was late, but your dad said you could stay until the end, because Campbells don't leave baseball games early. And Mauer hit a pop foul right to you. You didn't bobble it or anything. It fell into your hands like a gift. The people around you clapped. It was on the Jumbotron and everything! Some guy next to you said they could use you at shortstop. . . . And it was so late, but you and your dad waited outside after the game, and finally all the players came out, and you waited some more, and you practiced what you were going to say. And then Joe Mauer came out, and you just held out the ball to him, because you forgot how to speak English. And he smiled at you and asked you if he could sign your ball. And you just nodded like a big dork. And he did sign it and he told you to get some sleep, and you didn't let anyone else touch the ball and you looked up on the Internet how to preserve it best, and you didn't even let me touch it. And then . . . and then . . ." Hazel shook her head. She was crying now, and the tears burned her scar and bit at her face. "My dad left. . . . And I didn't know what to do. And you came over, and . . ."

Hazel dissolved. The words flew away. There was nothing. Jack looked down at the ball and squeezed it. He turned it around in his hands again.

And then he looked up and blinked.

"Hazel?"

Chapter Twenty-five

HAZEL AND THE WOODS

"Jack?"

He was squeezing the ball in one hand and staring at her. He was shuddering harder, now, and his skin shone as if he were sweating.

She could not move, she could not do anything but let the tears run down her cheeks and stare back at him, willing him back to her.

"Hazel," he repeated, like her name was a revelation. He blinked at her. "I gave you this."

"Yes."

He looked at the ball again, and then at her. "I'm really cold."

"I know," she said. She inhaled and her stomach

contracted. "Jack," she said, "we can go somewhere warmer. Would you like that?"

He blinked at her. "Yeah," he said.

"Okay," she said, and it was the only word she could say.

She crouched down next to Jack and put her arm around him. He was wet and so cold he felt wrong to her, and she had to work to suppress a shudder. Hazel wrapped both arms around him and pulled him into her. She'd never realized how skinny he was—but that was Jack, he burned off energy just by being alive. He shivered and shuddered and she tucked him into herself, though she was a very small girl. *I am warm,* she thought. *I am warm and I am getting warmer. I am gathering all the warmth of my body, of all the Hazels past and future, and I am giving it to you.*

She held him like that, willing him to leach warmth from her, willing his body to learn from the rhythm of her heartbeat, the steadiness of her breath.

Then the ground beneath them cracked. The sound hit the air like a slap. Freezing water crept onto Hazel's legs.

Hazel looked up. The ice floe they were on had split. Water as dark and sickly as the storm-tossed sky seeped onto their perch.

"Jack," she whispered. "We have to go. Come on." She was trying her best to sound brave and in control, because she was the one whose heart knew how to beat and lungs knew how to breathe and legs knew how to walk, and that passed for heroism now.

Hazel wiped her face and stood up, pulling Jack up with her. His legs sank, and she gasped and pulled him back up. "Can you walk?" she whispered, her heart squeezing.

He inhaled. "I think so," he said.

He drew himself up, clutching the baseball in his hand, with Hazel supporting him. The shift in weight caused the ice floe to dip into the black water, and Jack fell back down. Water splashed on him, and he flinched.

The floe was melting. Hazel's eyes snapped to the lake. Around them, the black water was stealthily infiltrating the ice.

"Come on," she said, tugging him up again.

With one arm on Jack's back and another supporting his chest, Hazel pushed him forward. The palace loomed east of them, but to the west was a line of trees. The woods, calling her back.

"This way," she said. They stepped from Jack's floe to the next one. Jack inhaled and looked behind him.

"What?" she said, turning to look. Jack's floe had cracked into four pieces now.

"Nothing," he said, his eyes on the ice behind him. "Come on."

Hazel could feel the water beneath their feet rocking,

roused like an awakening beast. The patch of ice rocked with it, and Hazel struggled to keep them both standing. Water lapped away at their perch. The next floe was a giant step away.

"We'll go at the same time," she whispered to Jack. "Ready?"

"Hazel," he said.

"It's okay, Jack," she said.

"Hazel!"

She looked up. Jack was staring off to the right. She followed his gaze and then sucked in a breath.

The palace loomed there watchfully. It was not alone. Standing in front of it, just before the shore of the lake, was the white witch.

Hazel had not realized how tall she was, how oddly thin she was, like a woman made of a cold breath. She seemed almost insubstantial, and yet she emitted a force that made you want to crawl toward her. She was a hundred yards away, but Hazel still felt the touch of those eyes on her. She wondered what the witch was thinking, and if she was impressed with Hazel for convincing Jack to go.

The witch did not step toward them, she did not call to them, she merely stood there, completely still, the center of this desolate universe, while the air bowed to her. Next to Hazel, Jack did not move. He looked at the white witch and

Hazel could tell he was making a home in her gaze.

The floe rocked. The water splashed at their feet. Hazel stumbled to the right, carrying Jack with her, and still he did not stop looking at the witch.

"Jack," she said, her voice a hiss. "Come on." She tugged at him, pulling him forward. "Big step now," she whispered, trying to keep her voice from shaking. She did not need to look to know the witch was standing there, perfectly erect, watching them. She could feel her presence, and Jack still could not take his eyes away. But he allowed himself to be pulled along as they lurched over the black crevice to the next floe, Hazel conscious of how clumsy she must look.

They stepped and the floe collapsed. Hazel lunged forward, feeling Jack slip out of her arms. She fell on a small piece of ice, smacking her face again. Her feet landed in the water, and a shock of cold ran through her body so intense she yelped. And then she heard another splash, a bigger one. Jack.

Hazel was alone on the small patch of ice, while freshly displaced water churned next to her. Hazel scampered over to the edge of the ice just as Jack's head burst through the water, eyes popping, his breath sucking in the sky. He threw himself toward the ice floe, and Hazel grabbed onto his left arm.

"It's okay, Jack," she said, panting. "I've got you."

It was only half true. In her mind she saw herself losing her grip, she saw Jack falling into the dark waters, she saw herself rescuing him from the ice only to lose him to something worse.

But Jack threw his right arm on the ice and Hazel helped him prop himself up. His face was white with shock. His chest was heaving frantically. The water had sucked away whatever warmth Hazel had given him. Hazel tugged on his arm and Jack wriggled his way up.

And then he was up and lying on the floe, shuddering.

And still the witch stood there, watching.

Hazel fell on top of him. "Jack, Jack, are you okay?"

He did not answer, only let out a small noise as chills racked his body and Hazel tried so desperately to give him warmth, there on top of the small patch of ice, while the water lapped hungrily at them.

The ice meant safety now, but it could only protect itself, for the water was coming. The ice surrendered bit by bit. Pieces cracked in front of them, and the dark water burst through the cracks. On her perch, Hazel could feel the water beneath her buzzing with greedy anticipation.

"Jack," she urged. "We have to go."

He did not talk, did not say a word, but he let her help him up. And then he froze and looked at his empty hand.

"The baseball," he breathed.

"Oh," said Hazel, heart plummeting. "The baseball."

The baseball was gone, consumed by the black waters. It seemed like just an ordinary thing, but it was a baseball, signed by Joe Mauer, and Jack had given it to her, and in that way it was magic.

"Jack, I'm sorry. We have to go. The ice is melting. Come on." She put her arms around him and led him still forward, though the ground heaved and disappeared beneath her feet. And the water roiled, and the witch watched on, and Hazel could hear the bells of her voice in her head: *Do you see, now, there are things worse than the ice. Do you see what happens when it melts? Do you see what you did?*

Hazel wondered what Jack was hearing. She could not tell, he was just a shivering shell of a boy. Hazel kept talking as they crept along—"Here, step here, be careful, don't slip"—and under her words hummed the whisper: *I'm here, I'm here.*

And then they were on the shore. Jack still said nothing, and there was nothing to do but trudge through the snow to the woods. Hazel kept her arms around Jack. He was still shuddering, and his muscles seemed only half there, like the rest of him was still on the ice. She kept pattering along, "Almost there, almost there, just a little farther." She didn't know if it was helping Jack, but it gave her some distraction from the things churning inside her.

And still he said nothing.

And then they were in front of the woods. And the witch was still there, still watching them, and though Hazel had survived it all, though she had Jack, though she was about to cross the woods to go back home, she still felt like she'd failed.

All you can do, the guard at the village had said, *is pretend she's not there.*

"We're going into the woods, now," Hazel whispered to Jack. "We're leaving." *Say something.*

He did not. Hazel inhaled and stepped into the trees, and though the gaze of the witch tugged at her she did not look back.

But she wanted to.

Jack's body tensed sharply as they entered the woods, and Hazel ignored it and moved on. The woods welcomed them back. There was no snowstorm, no churning sky, no assaulting cold on this side of the witch's palace. Maybe because no one had ever left before.

And there, the familiar sound: *Tick tock. Tick tock.* Hazel breathed it in.

And they went. Hazel dropped her hand and Jack walked on his own, though Hazel stayed close. The sun was rising in the sky, turning the snow on the ground to slush. It was warmer now, survivable. But Jack was still shuddering, still white, like the dark water still coursed in his veins.

"Let's just get ahead a bit," Hazel said. "It warms up soon."

It turned out she did not need the compass. It was easy to head in the other direction from the lair of the witch. All you had to do was move away from the thing pulling at you.

They walked up a gentle slope, moving through the trees. They did not talk to each other, but Hazel kept glancing at Jack, making sure he was still with her. He was, but barely. He seemed so focused on making his feet move like they were supposed to. And maybe that was all he wanted to think about.

Hazel wanted to ask him what he was thinking, what he was feeling, if he was regretting the witch or was just too tired to think, if he was embarrassed that the princess had rescued the knight or if he didn't mind so much now that it had happened, if he remembered everything that had passed, if he was mad at himself for going with the witch, if his warm blood was winning the battle against the water in his veins; she wanted to reach out and grab the things in his mind and heart and hold them so they could examine them together, but they were not hers to take.

So she led Jack along the cart path, following the sound of the clock and pulling away from the cold. The sun was being kind to Jack, warming him gently, giving him what Hazel could not. It was like they'd taken their planned trip into the woods—except then going home would have been as simple as following the breadcrumbs they'd scattered together.

Hazel followed the cart path and the sounds of the clock. The journey this way was easy, though she suspected the woods could lead her wherever they chose.

And they were done with her.

And she was done with them.

They rejoined the small footpath when the sun was near its peak in the sky and the woods was in full-on spring. The faint green smell in the air felt like an embrace. And then they entered the clearing with the clock.

It was a strange thing to stand there on the other end of the clearing where she'd stood at the beginning of all of this. The clock was still there, but it looked smaller now, and less odd—like every woods would have a skinned grandfather clock in it.

Her ravens were still there, whispering to each other. One of them croaked and nodded at her from across the field, and then at the clock face.

Hazel went up to look at the clock. It read 10:30. Judging by the height of the sun in the sky, that was in no way the time in the woods. The other raven trilled at her, and she got the distinct impression it was telling her she was an idiot. Hazel chewed on her lip, and then reached up and moved the clock's arms so it read 7:00, and switched the picture of the sun to the moon. Maybe it would work.

"We're almost there," she told Jack, guiding him out of the clearing.

Jack saw the wolf before she did, and he gasped and froze, pointing ahead. The wolf was just where she'd left him, standing sentry by a tree, watching out for intruders in the woods.

"What do we do?" Jack breathed. It was the first thing he'd said since losing the baseball.

"It's okay," Hazel said to Jack.

The wolf did not move, only blinked and sniffed the air. She nodded at it as they passed.

And then they were at the tree line, and Hazel exhaled. Jack looked at her, his brown hair as messy as always. Some things would never change.

"This is it," she said, because something needed to be said.

"That's home?" Jack asked, his voice soft.

"Yeah," Hazel said.

Jack looked at her, and then back at the woods. His shoulders fell. "I don't know," he said quietly.

"What? You don't know what?"

"I . . . don't know." His body twitched back toward the woods.

Hazel sucked in a breath. "You can't go back!"

"I know, I know. But"—he looked toward the world beyond the trees—"I don't know if I can do that, either." He shifted in his place.

"You can't stay here!" she said.

He gazed at her, his pale face serious and searching. "Why not?"

Hazel blinked. *Because I need you. Because you're my best friend. Because I have to go out there, too.*

"Because it's worse in here," she said.

Jack looked down. The green of the spring grass reached up to him. He took his hand and rubbed his chest, just where his heart was. He shifted again.

"I was mean to you," he said quietly.

"I know," Hazel said. It was on the tip of her tongue to say *It's okay,* except it wasn't, and he knew it.

"I don't know how to do things right sometimes."

Hazel glanced to the ground. "I don't either," she said.

"And Mom . . ." he said, and then looked away.

Hazel was supposed to say something comforting now, something that would let him know it was going to be okay, except she knew nothing of the kind. But that was still better than this.

"Come on," she said, and she tucked her hand through his arm. "We should go home."

Jack exhaled, and Hazel took that as agreement and pulled him through the trees. Hazel's foot landed in the snow and she muttered, "Oh, great." She was sick of winter.

It was dark out, and the air was filled with the squeals of sledding kids. It was the same scene that she'd left. A great fatigue slammed into Hazel, and with terrible dread she thought of the blocks they had to walk.

They crossed the street to the sidewalk. They'd made this walk hundreds of times in their lives together. It was as familiar as air.

There was so much she wanted to tell him. There had been wolves and weird psychics, swanskins and bird girls. There had been a marketplace that sold potions for forgetting, a wizard who could pull truths from your heart. There had been a cottage, a couple, a garden. There had been a match girl. There had been a journey. There was a witch who wanted nothing. And at the end of it all there was Jack, and maybe the witch was right, maybe things wouldn't be the same, but Hazel would still do everything she could to remind him what he was made of. There was so much she wanted to tell him—it used to be that nothing really happened to her unless she told Jack about it—but they walked in silence.

A minivan stopped in the street next to them, and a window rolled down to reveal the face of Tyler's mom. She called to them and motioned them into the car. "Come on, I'll drive you home!"

Jack and Hazel exchanged a look, shrugged, and climbed in the backseat.

Tyler was in the front, and he had turned fully around and was gaping at them. Hazel's hackles instinctively went up, and then she breathed them away. It wasn't going to be like that anymore. She wouldn't let it.

"Are you okay?" Tyler whispered to Jack.

Jack nodded slightly.

Hazel's eyes went to the dashboard of the minivan. It read 7:10.

"Is it still Friday?" she whispered to Tyler.

He nodded, wide-eyed. His eyes were on her face now, like they could not quite take in the magnitude of her scar. Hazel's hand flew to it and traced it all down the length of her cheek to her jaw.

"Hazel, what happened?" asked Mrs. Freeman, eyes full of alarm. "That looks fresh. Did someone do that to you?"

"Oh," said Hazel. "I tripped." What was she going to tell her mom? She had to think of something. She had to get used to the question.

"I see," said Tyler's mom, looking dubious. "And what

are you doing out without your coats? Jack, I thought you were with your elderly aunt Bernice?"

"What?" Jack said. Hazel elbowed him.

"He came back," said Hazel.

"Okay . . ."

Tyler's mom drove them the few blocks to their houses. When Hazel and Jack spilled out, Tyler was silent. His mother noticed. "Aren't you going to say good-bye to your friends?" Hazel heard her say as the two got out onto the sidewalk.

Tyler rolled down the window and called good-bye. He started to roll the window up and then stopped.

"Hey, Hazel?"

"What?"

"You can hang out with us at recess on Monday if you want."

And then he rolled up the window and they drove away, leaving Hazel and Jack standing in front of their houses.

"Um, everyone thinks you're with your aunt Bernice," Hazel said.

Jack looked at her, brown eyes wide. "I don't have an aunt Bernice," he said.

A light went on in Jack's house behind them. Hazel looked up toward it, and then back at Jack. Jack rubbed his hand against his chest.

His mom appeared on the stoop and Jack straightened. He looked at Hazel. "I should go."

She nodded.

"Hazel?"

"Yeah?"

"Thanks for coming to get me."

"Of course." She was his best friend.

Jack hesitated still, and Hazel wanted to say something comforting, give him some bright plastic flowers of words, but Jack would see them for what they were. Jack knew how to see things.

Then he put his hand up and squeezed her arm, and then turned toward his house. Hazel stood and watched him disappear inside.

Hazel went to her own front door and walked in, breathing in the smells of home. She called for her mother, but there was no answer. Of course not, her mom had her class. Hazel's heart sank a little. She would have liked to see her mom.

She thought about going to the kitchen and getting some food, but she couldn't bear the thought of the extra movements, so she went to her room to lie down on her bed.

Her stuffed animals were still there, sitting against her pillow, and Hazel lay down next to them and put her hand on the bear, then grabbed it and pulled it into her chest.

She tucked in a ball on her bed. Her eyes fell on the spot where the Joe Mauer baseball used to be. Maybe she would get Jack another signed ball. It might not be easy, but it had to be easier than this.

Then she noticed the wrapped present on her bed stand. She rolled over to grab it. The gift wrap was familiar—shiny purple paper that her mother had been using for six months. Hazel unwrapped the paper to reveal an old shoe box. She opened up the box and unfolded the tissue paper inside to find a pair of pink ballet shoes.

She blinked and picked up one of the shoes. There was a note in the tissue paper:

Hazel—

A present and a promise.

Love,

Mom

The writing blurred in front of Hazel's eyes. She touched the note with her fingers. She wanted to get up and leave her mom a note, but she could not leave the bed. So Hazel took both slippers and folded them in her arms with the teddy bear and curled back up on the bed. She could see the distant glow from Jack's house coming in the window, and she wondered what he was doing, and if he was okay, and if he'd eaten, and what he'd told his parents. She wondered what things would be like between them now, and what she was going to have to do for them to be normal again. It would be harder to watch over him if they weren't normal, but she would find a way. She wondered if she'd actually want to hang out with Tyler and Bobby at recess. Maybe a little capture the flag would do them all good. Hazel was good at capture the flag. No one took her seriously because she was small and feathered, a strange little dino-bird, but she had a sickle claw and she was not afraid to use it.

Once upon a time, there was a boy named Jack who got lost in the woods. His best friend went after him. Along the way, she had many adventures. She met woodsmen, witches, and wolves. She found her friend in the thrall of a queen who lived in a palace of ice and had a heart to match. She rescued him with the help of a magical object. And they returned home, together, and they lived on, somehow, ever after.

It went something like that, anyway.

She drifted off to sleep thinking that tomorrow, she would call Adelaide and make plans to go over there. This time she would bring her own ballet shoes. She wanted to tell Adelaide and Uncle Martin all about the Snow Queen. They probably wouldn't believe her, not really. She wouldn't believe it herself.

But at least it was a good story.

Anne Ursu is the author of the three middle-grade novels that comprise the Cronus Chronicles trilogy: *The Shadow Thieves*, *The Siren Song*, and *The Immortal Fire*. She is also a professor of writing for children at Hamline University and a lifelong Minnesota Twins fan. Anne lives in Minneapolis with her son and three cats.

For exclusive information on your favorite authors and artists, visit www.authortracker.com.

Also available as an ebook.